# Masquerade of Evil

## Edwina Groat

ISBN: 978-1-955622-49-3

PUBLISHED BY

Fideli Publishing, Inc.
119 W. Morgan St.
Martinsville, IN 46151

www.FideliPublishing.com

PRINTED IN THE UNITED STATES OF AMERICA

# Prologue

The ancient one lay down in the coolness of God's great cavern. He was weary and troubled by the non-believer known as Harry Quinn, the human he had left behind in his last encounter with the Evil One. Harry Quinn was a force of good that needed to be preserved.

Harry Quinn's future was filled with uncertainty and danger. Trouble lay ahead of him. He will need protection through spiritual power.

He was worth the effort.

# Chapter 1

Harry Quinn was in love. He was no kid. For the first time in his forty-two years, he found himself almost speechless as he shook her hand on introduction. No one was more surprised than Harry. He had given up on the love concept long ago. Now as he stared into her soft green eyes, it was the sensation of an express elevator going down. She was a redhead, and her name was Maureen Brady. Her skin was alabaster and her voice was soft but spoke with a crisp clear resonance from rosebud lips beneath an almost perfect nose befitting her face. Harry Quinn was toast. After retrieving his insides from the unexpected descent, he invited her to please have a seat. Tiffany had made the appointment last week with Ms. Brady, who had indicated she may need some surveillance and the services of a private investigator. Mr. Quinn had come highly recommended by her attorney Joshua Lawton. Harry must remember to call Josh to express his thanks.

Ms. Brady was frightened. She first emphasized her reluctance in coming here. Knowing of course her story was too bizarre to be believable. Maureen had been down that road before, it was only when the stress on her became unbearable that she went to Josh Lawton, her uncle's attorney. She knew a psychiatrist or the police could not help her. Maureen was not dealing with psychosis or delusions; this was a very clear and present evil to her. Harry listened, and after his assurance of confidence, she condensed her story as best she could. Feeling foolish, she confessed it was more of a feeling than hard evidence. Maureen was not an only child; she had a sister. A twin. They were both gainfully employed at the moment. Thirty-six and comfortable. Maureen was an executive buyer for Saks Fifth Avenue, never married, had no children, and loved her job. She was a workaholic and lived comfortably within her means.

Her sister Nora had been married twice and divorced, for reasons Nora never quite explained to Maureen. Both husbands had left her with nothing and in debt, so she said. Nora was currently working as a receptionist in a prominent plastic surgeon's office she lucked into, after quickly going through three other jobs within the year. Not exactly the income to sustain her lifestyle. Harry was hoping this would all come to a point, but he didn't care. He sat there consumed by the story and her clear soft voice.

Harry offered a glass of water and waited for her to continue. She hesitated and added a younger brother named Conrad to her tale, which she reluctantly admitted was worthless. He had been in and out of trouble since he was a teen. He had been a good kid and had a promising athletic career, but somewhere along the line, he seemed to have lost his way. She had loaned him money, lied for him, and put him up when he needed a roof over his head when he was too drunk to go to their uncle's house.

Maureen and her siblings had lost their parents to a boating accident during a fluke storm off the coast of South Carolina. The boat capsized, and both bodies recovered, leaving the teens with no life insurance, and a home with a mortgage. They moved in with her father's older brother in their teens.

Maureen loved her uncle, as he did all his deceased brother's children, he was childless and recently lost his wife. Maureen moved out after college, came back after Nora married, went through two marriages, and returned home. Conrad never left. She paused; she had gone on far too long without getting to the point.

Harry prompted her, "Ms. Brady, you must tell me why you think I can help you."

"I'm here because of a premonition, Mr. Quinn, I'm not crazy. All those things you hear about twins are true. My uncle is a very wealthy man, a good and loving man. I love him. Something terrible is going to happen. I fear for his life. This is not just a whim. Thoughts and visions have been nagging me for weeks. I'm at the end of my rope. I couldn't rest anymore." Harry surmised the rest.

"And you feel your sister may harm him, or worse?"

Funny, that was the first thing that came to Harry's mind. Finally, it was out. Maureen had put into words; her premonition. Her vision.

"Not just my sister Mr. Quinn. I think my brother may be in on it too, I don't know."

The visions came to her in short, staccato blips. Her siblings were planning her uncle's death. Once she heard her own words out loud conveyed to another human being, a visible serenity came over her. She had been harboring these feelings for weeks and did not know where or who to turn to, certainly not the police. They would not take her seriously, and she definitely could not confront her sister.

Harry was not quite sure that HE took her seriously, but he did assure her, he would help her, if he could, no promises. He hadn't the foggiest notion of what to do in a situation like this. These were unchartered waters. Harry's strong demeanor and soft reassuring words seemed to comfort her.

As she rose to leave, she was far more at ease, leaving behind her that frenzied look of someone who just awoke from a bad dream. Maybe that's all it was. A bad dream, and she just needed someone to vent her fears and frustrations. She did not seem the type that needed to seek professional counsel. Ms. Brady appeared to be self-assured and strong, after unburdening herself of her private thoughts. It took some kind of confidence to reach out to someone with such an outlandish story. She reached out to shake his hand and thank him as she left.

Harry, again, was on that express elevator. He held onto her hand a bit too long and caught himself. He could have stared into those soft green eyes forever.

Recovering, he opened his office door and led her to the outer office and past Tiffany. She briefly acknowledged Harry's associate and thanked her also, Tiffany nodded and smiled, as she noticed her boss being unduly chivalrous. As he closed the door behind Maureen, he promised he would be in touch. He turned and noticed a wicked grin on his girl Friday.

"Hmmm, you've become quite the "Sir Walter Raleigh."

"Oh shut up," he playfully retorted. "I was just being a gentleman. Why? Isn't that allowed anymore?" He gave her that broad movie star grin and disappeared behind his office door.

# Chapter 2

Are you out of your mind Harry? How do you investigate a premonition? The logical, no-nonsense Harry was being heard from at three o'clock in the morning. How could a tough guy detective like you be taken in by a pair of green eyes? You should have politely escorted her out and refused to handle such an absurd request.

"Yes. Yes, I know, he muttered, to no one in particular, as he shooed this thing called Better Judgement away. He could not sleep! The green eyes and her obvious distress would not allow him. Whatever happened to a good old-fashioned missing person's case, or who killed uncle Leroy, or Mrs. Baker's missing jewels. Harry was used to high-profile cases, insurance fraud, syndicated break-ins, cold case files, the unsolved ones the cops could not crack. Of all things, Josh had done it to him again. The last things he checked out for Josh were ghostly apparitions and fairy tale goblins surrounding the Averys' old renovated house. Now he's got me chasing psychic nonsense. Begrudgingly sleep overtook him and Harry dozed off in a restless state until the quiet of the morning was cut short by his alarm.

Harry waltzed through talk radio news, performing his well-organized morning ritual. He chose per usual one of his finely tailored suits, this one a dark blue subdued herringbone. Accompanied by a gleaming white slightly starched shirt with cufflinks. The blue-sky silk tie offset his striking blue eyes. When Harry walked into a room, all heads turned, from his highly polished shoes to the tip of his slightly graying head. Harry Quinn usually had it all together, the way he ate, drank, slept, and generally led his life. He was a measured man in all manner of thought and deed, and yet this morning as he left for the office, he felt at odds with everything. He knew it was leftover stirrings from the woman who entered his life yesterday.

# Chapter 3

Seemingly bewitched, Harry found himself driving out of the city's unrelenting cacophony of moving parts and noises heading for an address Ms. Brady had given him for her uncle. He was in no hurry and the big black 760 BMW held steady and purposely to the interstate. This was Harry's thinking time. Given the nature of this assignment, he was at odds as to how to approach his subject with such an absurd warning. Research on Mr. John Brady revealed a man in his mid-60's healthy, athletic, self-made. His business consisted of about 30 employees of his mid-size aeronautical supply company, a portion of which was funded and begun by a gizmo he had patented as a young engineer thirty years ago which somehow improved the sound and circulation system of the aircraft. His business background was clean. He had a reputation as a straight shooter, no bs.

Mr. Brady's employees held him in high regard and for all practical purposes, he loved dogs and helped all old ladies across the street. Tiffany was never known, NOT to be thorough. Harry seemed to have an accurate grasp of the man he was about to meet. It was a Sunday afternoon and Harry knew he was taking a chance the man he was appraising in his mind would not be home. His decision to take this thing head-on may not work, he was about to find out. The impromptu visit from a total stranger with a professional air and who addressed the immediacy of the need to talk may have helped to convince Mr. Brady this is no joke, though Harry had not fully convinced himself it was legitimate.

He found the address he was looking for chiseled neatly on one of two gated columns. The gates were open, and after negotiating a beautifully landscaped shaded driveway, Harry found himself parked under an arched entrance to one of the older Long Island homes. It was well maintained in a natural state, and not overly manicured. He noticed the date of 1920 on the cornerstone. Climbing the three steps between two large potted plants, he knocked on the oversized arched door sporting a small window covered in ornate twisted bars. After briefly seeing a face in the window, the man himself answered. It was clear this man was inline blood to the woman he met yesterday. The kinship could not be denied. Green eyes met Harry's gaze, directly and honestly, and the aura surrounding him exuded a no-nonsense character. His face was patrician, and his jaw locked firmly beneath the broad forehead of an aristocrat. ** His demeanor was civil, but a bit puzzled. It was obvious he did not receive visits such as this too often.

"Mr. Brady?" No response. "Mr. John Brady?"

While Mr. Brady digested the question with hesitancy, Harry pulled out his credentials and identifications, a practice that became second nature to him over his eight years at the DC swamp bureau. Harry understood the furrowed brow of mistrust, as John Brady studied his credentials and finally answered "yes, how may I help you?"

"Mr. Brady, my name is Quinn, I'm here representing someone who has your best interest at heart. This visit is not to alarm you, only to speak to you out of concern."

At that moment the unmistakable sound of a sports classic roared in and parked behind Harry's BMW. Tanned and toned, a thin blond-haired young man carelessly put together jumped casually from the driver's seat, quickly eyed the two men up and down, dismissed Harry as inconsequential, and flippantly acknowledged his uncle as he breezed through the front door. This Harry thought, had to be the worthless brother, Conrad.

After recovering from the disdain left in Conrad's wake. Harry asked that he may speak in private. With a noticeable weary look of frustration on Conrad's arrival, Mr. Brady regained his composure, invited Harry in, and led him to his study. The office and study be-fit the man. It was the old-world charm, smelling of leather and highly polished wood. Oils of gentlemen at The Hunt were displayed over the mantle of the stone fireplace and lush landscapes and river scenes graced a wood-planked wall distinguished by its aged patina. There was a painting of a woman with a large dog at her feet displayed behind him at his desk, and on the far wall, it seemed it was the business he ran with his employees as it grew over the years. All his trinkets and treasures were spread around him in carefully chosen places.

Offhandedly, Harry offered his compliments of the Brady home and surroundings, while he mentally took note of the man's office. Years in this business sharpened his trusting nature. Before Mr. Brady could offer him a seat, Harry noted the gardens outside; the two large glass arched doors leading to the gardens.

"Mr. Brady, would you mind? I noticed your beautiful gardens. May we speak outside?" Harry had struck a nerve, John Brady's slight irritation lifted.

"It was my wife's passion."

For a few brief moments, John Brady pointed out some of the highlights of his wife's handiwork as they strolled down a brick pathway, but his patience grew thin. Harry finally heard John Brady ask in a strong no-nonsense voice.

"What's this all about Mr. Quinn?"

Harry took a deep breath. "I'm really not quite sure why I'm here. The urgency in my client's voice and genuine concern for your welfare prompted my coming here. They only would say they felt you needed to know that there are forces that are, shall we say "unfriendly" toward you." Brady was caught up in genuine disbelief.

"Do you know of any enemies you might have or business situations that went sour, any reason at all that would provoke harm to you? Do you trust your staff? Any new personnel?"

The fact that anyone in his business or personal life would do him harm was completely foreign to him.

"Look, Mr. Brady, I assure you that I am not used to requests like this. I deal in facts, assist with the authorities when necessary, involve myself with insurance fraud, and deal with Real crimes. It was at the request of a friend that I came here regarding this client. The plea for your safety was sincere and real, and again anonymous."

The threat to his safety was beginning to take hold as the furrowed look of concern replaced his displeasure at this interruption on Sunday afternoon.

"I must also ask that you speak to no one about this, no one. I would think about installing a security system and having your premises swiped for any devices. If anyone asks, my reason for being here is simply a review of your insurance policies and ways to improve cost efficiency. Mr. Brady If you think of anything," Harry pulled out his card and handed it to him. "Please call me, John," he offered. "John," Harry returned the overture. "Call me anytime, if you feel or suspect something is not right or think of anything you have overlooked. Call."

Somewhere within the short walk down the garden path, Harry Quinn had gained John Brady's trust. He liked the man and would be unhappy to see any harm come to him. He said his goodbyes and continued down the path past the greenhouse and out the gate.

# Chapter 4

Conrad Brady followed the black BMW until it left his sight. He was unfamiliar with the car and indeed the person he quickly noted as he came home this afternoon. He was familiar with the comings and goings of people coming around his uncle's home. Conrad had much more time to observe such things since his uncle had relieved him of any duties at his company warehouse. He was still smarting at his uncle John's observation of his work habits and his obvious disappointment and his lack of enthusiasm for the tasks that were assigned to him. That was OK with him. He hated the job, and the people his uncle surrounded him with. It was only a temporary thing anyway until Conrad figured out his "calling".

He was tall, blond, and good-looking. Girls couldn't get enough of him in college, and he was athletic enough to be a star quarterback in high school and college, but not enough to cut it in the big time. He had tried out for the New York Jets, The Dolphins, and The Cowboys, but at 27 his California surfer boy and big-time athletic star image had started to fade. Conrad had decided he was not going to end up wasting away wrapped up in one of his uncle's engineering mechanical lines.

His college and football funding from his uncle had run its course and the only money he could expect from him now was, well nothing, since his hostile and hasty retreat from his uncle's firm. He was lucky to have a roof over his head. He couldn't even buy a beer for friends at the club since his uncle had put a limit on his charges there and he was warned about the usage of his uncle's credit card. Things were starting to look bleak for Conrad the super-star. Things had to change and pretty soon.

Conrad wondered if he had put the same restrictions on Nora. She was due home anytime. Nora was his best sounding board and advice giver. He had no plans for tonight, most of his college colleagues had pockets full of cash and real jobs. He could tell his brand of entertainment to regale all with old football stories that were not even worth another round for the table. His overnight crashes and weekly hang-around with friends were losing their luster like the proverbial three-day-old fish.

Tonight, he was forced to stay here. Even the ladies seemed to have tired of his charm. So, he poured himself a drink of Uncle John's finest scotch and nestled himself down at the pool surrounded by Uncle John's lovely garden and waited for sis to tell him what an awful day she had at work.

Her tales of woe could only make him feel better, and of course, his sympathetic ear was ever tuned in to her self-pitying and indulgent, I deserve better attitude. These two siblings were certainly unhappy and misunderstood people.

They sat and chatted for hours wallowing in each other's misery. It was only when her self-pity and his validation for that self-pity led to an evening ending in uncontrollable laughter and an alcoholic high. It is true misery loves company, but when a bartender named "Validation" shows up, he's apt to serve a very toxic cocktail.

# Chapter 5

It was an early call, shortly before eight when Maureen answered. Harry had called her at the office. His take on the lady told him she would be there first thing in the morning. He was pleased she answered the phone and welcomed his call. The thought of her, and hearing that caressing voice had completely undermined his decision to be all business and professional.

Instead of reporting to her on the phone about his meeting with her uncle, he found himself asking her to meet him for lunch at a small café not too far from her office. Without hesitancy, she agreed to meet him at noon. In the ensuing hours, Tiffany devilishly taunted Harry's unrealistically "fine mood" he was in. He was always in a good mood but this particular morning Tiffany noticed her boss being noticeably preoccupied.

"Oh Harry, again Oh Harry," she cooed. She felt she was reeling a kite in, caught up in a wayward wind. The outside view of a perfect day had wooed him into parts unknown. He landed with a start when he heard Tiff render her earth to Harry byline. With a start, he looked at her when she announced Josh was on the line.

"Oh, sorry he mumbled," as he picked up the receiver. "Hey, Josh, how are you? Want you to know that I received a client on your recommendation. Yes. Yes. Does Maureen Brady ring a bell? Um-Hmm.. is this another Devil in the cellar thing? Where do you get these people? You've got me chasing boogiemen and ghosts and now it's premonitions and visions. What have you gotten me into?"

"Harry, I would not have asked you had it not been her uncle being a client of the firm for many years. When she came to me, she was seriously upset but secretive. I assured her if she needed anonymity or privacy, she could talk to you with full confidence. I met Maureen a couple of times when she came with her uncle to the office. John had fractured his arm and she was helping him until he was able to drive. I hope you can help her, Harry". "I'll do my best Josh" Harry assured Josh he would help, if he could without revealing the devastating effect this woman had on him. "Anyway, Harry, I'm calling about an insurance situation. A client of mine was relieved of fifteen and a half million worth of jewels. Police have no leads. I'll email you the particulars." "Oh, the lady preferred emeralds."

"Ok Josh once I review, I'll call. Hey, end of the month poker game at Garth's. Ready to lose some money? Girls are taking a spa day."

"We'll see. I'm just ashamed to take advantage of a novice."

Harry hung up the phone and realized their good-natured sparring had brought him closer to his time to meet Maureen. He practically did a pirouette through the outer door as he winked at Tiffany and told her to take the rest of the day off. Tiffany had worked for this man for ten years and never saw this side. What had happened to her big tough detective boss. It couldn't be just any woman, he had plenty of those.

It had to be that woman. She couldn't be happier for him as she locked the door behind her, vaguely remembering there was a sale at Nordstrom.

# Chapter 6

Harry had perched himself outside under an umbrella. He had known this café and its owner in its infancy. It always had good food and good service. It had evolved over the years attracting a little more than the beer and chili set. But now, women and men executives pick up a quick bite as they added barreled greenery, waiters in black vests, and fru-fru bar drinks. Harry's world had gone al fresco. As high noon approached, he noticed her walking towards him with a smile and an extended hand. He immediately arose, took her hand, and thanked her for coming.

The warmth of her grasp sent kid-like fissures of giddiness through him. Her ability to take his breath away unnerved him. After staring into her eyes for a few brief seconds, he knew he could not treat this one with pure professionalism. Her beauty and nearness intimidated him, a human sensation that was foreign to him.

After a few awkward remarks about the weather and food served here, he offered his own straightforward approach to the problem she had presented him.

"I saw your uncle yesterday. I drove to his residence on the chance that he may be home and I would have the ability to meet the man face to face. I introduced myself and told him directly my reason for being there. There was annoyance and puzzlement at first, but at the end of our conversation Your Uncle John began to realize the seriousness of my visit, and that this was not a prank. Your name and who you are were never divulged. Your uncle only knows that I was contacted by an anonymous source who felt that his well-being is at risk. I continued to probe, asking if he had any enemies or competitors in his field that may want to do him harm. You do know Maureen, your uncle is highly regarded by his business associates and employees, and friends. John has nothing but the highest respect from his immediate circle.

With that news, a broad smile spread across that incredible mouth of hers.

"Everyone loves Uncle John. Mr. Quinn, it's only my brother and sister I fear in these awful visions."

"I realize that Ms. Brady, but I could not tip my hand about the concern for your siblings, per your instruction. However, he is now alert to the fact that someone may have it in for him. I instructed him to speak to no one about our meeting and suggested he install a security system and surveillance around the house. My visit there was for updating and upgrading insurance for cost-efficiency for home and business if anyone should ask.  He has my card. I think I have his trust. I asked him to please call anytime day or night if anything seemed suspicious or out of the ordinary. He took me at my word, we shook hands and I left, knowing he was far more informed than before I came. You will get a full written report of this, but I did want to speak to you while my meeting with him was still fresh."

"Thank you. Mr. Quinn." "Please call me Harry,"

"Alright Harry," she said, as those soft green eyes swallowed him up in a sanctuary of pure pleasure.

She, again, voiced her very real concern about the when and how the devil's handiwork from her siblings may be handed out, even if her uncle was aware he was in danger. Harry assured her he would call John soon, do a little more research on the brother and her sister, and see if he could turn up anything else regarding their lifestyle outside the Brady home.

They stayed long after the luncheon rush had left with little snippets of information about each other, and when she got up to leave, he rose, took her hand again, and stiffly asked if she might have dinner with him sometime. The long lingering look from her and that curious look under her brow thought for a moment, and then said, "That would be nice"

As she turned to go, a hint of gardenia was left in her wake. Harry again found himself on that express elevator going down.

As she left, he summoned the waitress and ordered a double Chivas Regal on the rocks.

# Chapter 7

ow you've done it, Harry. You've really done it. The old sobering Harry came calling, with hard spun wisdom and no-nonsense attitude. He was not used to this. Harry was always in control. He lingered at the café and found himself enjoying the afternoon. The people, sounds, and sights around him brought him pleasure. He managed to dismiss Sobering Harry for the afternoon, paid the waitress, and tipped her lavishly.

This day felt different! It was a day to play hooky. A long time had passed since Harry enjoyed the day just for being the day. The sun was high and pleasurable and Harry found himself walking to Josh's office. He gave his most charming greeting to Josh's receptionist and walked in unannounced when told he was with no one. "Hiya kid.  He plopped himself down on the edge of the desk feigning his most endearing private eye attitude.

"So, you "lookin' to lose some money at poker this weekend?"

"Bring it on Bogie, there's always room for one more sucker,"

The playful banter went on until Josh finally took notice of a Harry he did not usually see.

"What's gotten into you today?"

What? Other than the fact I've had two double Chivas under my belt, and not long ago I had lunch with the lady Maureen you sent over. Josh, you've really gotten me into some silly situations, but this one has me up against a wall. I have absolutely nothing to go on but her so-called premonitions." "Well, she didn't go into a lot of detail with me, Harry. But enough to know you may be able to help her."

"I've never known you to turn tail on a case, Harry. C'mon it's more than that."

Josh took a closer look at this unconventional and mellow Harry he had never seen, and the lights came on!

"You LIKE her." Harry looked affronted. "Come on, flatfoot your smitten."

There was an actual flush to Harry's cheeks that was not a result of the Chivas.    "What have you done to me, kid?" he muttered to himself.

"I've never met anyone like her."

Both men laughed approvingly when Josh's assistant interrupted with copies he had requested. Josh thanked her and all laughter was gone, he handed them to Harry. Hope you can come out of the clouds long enough to check this out.

The file contained all particulars regarding the $15,500,000,00 worth of missing emeralds they spoke briefly of earlier that day. The victim Mrs. Juliet Breckenridge had just recovered from surgery at home and ended up in the hospital. She was widowed, in her sixties, and was recovering from a very nasty blow to the head. The police have nothing, no leads, nada. The insurance Co. wants to go all out on this one. Sobriety recaptured the room and Harry was again in bloodhound mode.

It was after 5:00 when Harry left Josh's office. He checked in briefly with Tiffany and caught a taxi home. Dinner consisted of pizza delivered and cold beer. For the next two hours, he poured over the file, but could not stay focused. He tuned into his recordings of Dashiel Hammet's Nick and Nora

Charles, and Sam Spade, famous detectives of the '30s.

The sophisticated Nick Charles had just solved another one for the bungling inept police as Harry fell asleep unraveling the mysteries of the Lost Emerald Caper. God how Harry loved those old movies.

# Chapter 8

Conrad counted twenty-five crisp one hundred dollar bills he had pulled out of a blank envelope. He caressed the bills as he inhaled the particular odor of the freshly minted bills. Sis had done it again. Nora had come through. When he was down to his last nickel, and no sign of employment in sight, she had found a quick easy job, No Questions Asked. That was OK with him. Conrad did not want to dirty his hands or know anything about anything. What he was asked to do was simple enough. He was to wait and drive. If he noticed anyone coming, he was to call. All simple enough. He knew whatever it was they were doing couldn't possibly be legal. But he didn't care. He was just there to drive. $2,500 was not bad for being a chauffeur for one night. Conrad never asked Nora any questions. With her, you just grabbed the money and ran, the less you knew the better off you were. Nora seemed to have a penchant for meeting the borderline type guys since college. She was like a cat with too much curiosity.

Conrad could remember Maureen begging Nora to stay away from that type. More than once he and his friends had to rescue his older sister from bad-boy types. She had a tendency to drink too much and talk too much. Hopefully, she will keep this job and find herself a substantial meal ticket. They were both getting too old for college shenanigans. Maureen was the smart twin. She had her life together and was happy with it.

Conrad respected Maureen, he did learn from her to stay away from the sleazy side of life. It was a road that led nowhere but to a bad end. He had no intentions of crossing the line dealing with low-life types, but Nora couldn't seem to stay away from it. Nora always had a hidden agenda, and after she came back from the failed marriages, she always managed to get him involved in her schemes as her sidekick.

After dealing with his glory days of being almost an NFL star, respected and loved, he found it demeaning and humiliating that his Uncle would expect him to start at the bottom of the business, sweeping warehouse floors and working on production lines. This entitlement attitude was fostered by Nora. She had convinced him he deserved to be wealthy and respected.

The old man shouldn't have given up on him so soon, a decision Conrad Brady was told his uncle would regret. No sir, Conrad Brady was not going to end up in an orange jumpsuit and poor.  He was talented and had plenty to offer. He was smart and was still holding out for the right offer. His athletic ability was still viable for the right team. He would continue to pick up a few dollars from her until things broke for him. It just seemed he was denied the right opportunity these last couple of years. He vowed to change the hand that life had dealt him.

# Chapter 9

The ancient one lay quietly on the hilltop. He had watched Harry leave the previous day. It was good that Harry, the non-believer, was to cross paths with John Brady. Evil had come to this place, and the power was growing. The Dark One had laid seed in the offspring of John Brady's brother. And now that his brother was gone, his choice to take the children in had put himself and family in eternal danger and damnationion. The Dark One's child had returned, the one called Nora. Redemption would never follow this one. Her failure and destruction of two marriages far from here had led her full circle back to John Brady's home. Were it not for the goodness of this man, she would have spread her vileness closer to the Dark One's own minions

Nora's attempt to steal John's treasure and soul would not be allowed, and Harry Quinn, the non-believer, was sent by the Divine Province to help Invictus protect John Brady and his family.

The great beast raised his head skyward on this cool soft day, surveilling his surroundings. His eyes and instincts keenly alert to any encroaching danger.It was the Lord's day, and peace and sanctity of his creation on this day allowed Invictus repose. He needed his rest. Evil was coming, and not too far in the future.

The great white wolf stretched languidly and closed his eyes. Secure rest did not always come so easily.

# Chapter 10

It was early when Harry received John Brady's call.

"I took your advice, Harry." John Brady now sounded like an old friend when he spoke.

"It was a wireless alarm system I had installed, but I had them check all rooms in the house. They found a camera and listening device in my office. That sixth sense of yours paid off. I have no idea how long it's been there."

"Actually, John, I'm sorry to hear that. It does prove, though, there is something to what my client claims regarding your safety. You must be on the alert now. Take nothing for granted such as packages, suspicious phone calls, or invites. Anything that may be out of the ordinary for you. Do not find yourself alone at your office, or anyplace else. Just stay alert to unusual circumstances.

We're all flying blind here John. The only facts we have here are whispers in the dark and glimpses in somebody's head. But it was still enough for a caring person to feel you should be warned. And again, I repeat tell no one, from your office or your immediate family. This all may be precautionary nonsense. But finding the camera and bug tell me there may be something to this client's concern. I know this has got to be a hell of a way to live, but for now, let me know of any changes in your routine."

"I feel better for your suggestion, Harry. I don't want my family in danger. My nephew and niece live here with me, and I in no way want them involved in any of this. I just would like to know who the hell if anyone I've crossed."

"Remember John this all may be a wild goose chase."
"Well, whatever it is, I have a security system now. The camera and bug they found were of the newer variety. Whoever put it there had to be within the last year."

"John, hold on to what they removed, I'll pick it up and see what I can come up with."

"Thanks, Harry," and hung up.

God, he felt like Benedict Arnold. How do you tell a guy his biggest suspect was his niece and nephew that

Maureen saw in a vision?  Crazy!  That sixth sense of Harry's was kicking in again.

It was time Harry had an opportunity to meet the family.

# Chapter 11

The green fire that splintered through the facets of the bracelet, momentarily had Nora mesmerized. The sun had hit the stone at just the right angle while Nora admired it. She was overwhelmed when her new beau of six months surprised her at dinner.  He was 10 years her junior, handsome, dark, and brooding, seemed to travel in all the right circles, and did all the right things in bed. The memory faded from when she had been showered with such attentiveness. He filled the void of the unhappy lifestyle she had since moving back with her uncle.

She was tired of her uncle and tired of his rules and hated living with him every minute of the day. The only interest Nora Brady had in her uncle was his money and a rather lavish place of residency.

After the second marriage collapsed, Uncle John reluctantly took her back into his home. She had turned down offers of college, work in his office, refused to change her lifestyle, embarrassed him with her drunken friends, and maxed out John's credit cards she borrowed. Nora pretty well figured he would not be paying for a third wedding. She was banned from bringing anyone to the house, and she was tired of trying to win his respect.

The green stones flashed fire again and brought her back to her evening with Johnny. They met casually at a trending water hole for all up-and-coming executives. For now, it was the place to be. His interest at first seemed tepid, however, the more they chatted the more Johnny hung on every word. Nora loved to talk about herself and the bad breaks that life had dealt her. She found Johnny to have a sympathetic ear, and he was quite charming in his appreciation of her good looks and interesting conversation. Last night was perfect, the roses, the fine dining, and the bracelet for the celebration of their six-month anniversary.

It was a magical evening. Perhaps there was a ring in her future. He had become the love of her life. And Johnny hung on to her every word.

# Chapter 12

Harry had called Maureen and asked that he might see her tonight for dinner. There were things he needed to talk to her about. He also made it quite clear that this was not all about business, that he was looking forward to her company. He was like a kid again, he actually found himself preening in front of the mirror, checking out the condition of his forty-two-year-old physique, grey hairs, and chin line. After moments of a thorough inspection, he winked at the mirror image looking back at him and gave a nod of approval.

Harry had remained lean and trim over the years, any hint of a gut invading that military cut body of his had little chance of remaining after Harry's onslaught of extra push-ups, sit-ups, and culinary caution. He enjoyed his beer, pizza, and good food. But as with everything else in his life, it was balanced and in order.

He shaved as he always had from his youth, with his old-fashioned blade and mug. As the razor swiftly glided through his many face contortions, he found his thoughts reluctantly turned to Maureen, her green eyes and soft voice. Splashing cold water over his finished product. He toweled off that square jaw and ran his hand over his handiwork to see that he did not miss a whisker. He carefully picked the right tie, the right shirt, and his best cuff-links. Dashed a bit of English Leather over his freshly shaven face, combed his hair, and slipped on his highly polished Alan Edmonds.

Satisfied with his sartorial splendor, he nervously checked the time and as if rehearsing for a school play, went over the lines he was going to say to Maureen. God, he hadn't felt this way since his high school prom.

She met him in the lobby of her apartment building. A very mellow and accommodating fellow announced his arrival at the front desk. When she emerged from the elevator Harry thought she had arrived by cumulus cloud surrounded by harp music.

He approached her, took her hand, and offered her a single rose. So far, so good Harry, you are doing fine. She smiled at him, accepted her rose, and allowed him to hurry her along to what he called a well-planned dinner for her, adding carefully, I hope you like Italian. Smiling broadly, she admitted she was starving and Italian was her favorite.

The evening started out on a high note, and Harry desperately wanted to get to what he and her uncle found, out of the way.

When they reached the restaurant, Harry got right to it. Looking at her directly he relayed the fact that her uncle had found surveillance equipment in his study.

"Your uncle was completely in the dark regarding his safety. At least now he is more aware of his surroundings, and he has no idea that it was you who came to me. Frankly, I found myself unable to accept such, what I thought, to be a preposterous claim. The fact that John found the listening device changed my attitude. I think it is about time I met your brother and sister.

I feel like a traitor unable to tell your uncle about his source of concern. In the meantime, he is going to be thinking about all past business transactions and anyone that may have a reason for harm to come to him. For now, anyone close or in the family knows that he is reviewing his insurance coverage and doing a cost analysis, so to speak. Next week I would like to arrive and meet the family."

Maureen listened silently and patiently and remarked that she was highly relieved that Harry did take her seriously. She thanked him for his thoroughness.

They both put business aside and vowed to enjoy the rest of the evening.

# Chapter 13

Johnny Polo had a tiger by the tail, and Johnny Polo was not stupid. He usually kept a very low profile of his unsavory business of choice. Burglary. His business dealings were clean, quick, In and out. No fuss, no bother. His hits would contact the insurance companies, and that would be that. He would never hit an area too much, he would carefully ration his skills at break-ins, nothing at random, and all very well thought out.

He had hit the mother-lode. Johnny popped the jeweler's loupe from his squinting eye, marveling at the quality of the stones. He expected a handsome haul, but nothing like this. They were all emeralds. Nora said she was crazy about emeralds. Stones like these were a collection that had names, like The Hope diamond, The Star of India The Agha Khan. The emerald he held in his hand was 9-10 carats, and in fact, the Jewel collection did have a name. "Satan's Fire".

The Breckenridge woman's private collection had just been returned from a showing in Beverly Hills, California while she was here on her third facelift at the plastic surgeon where Nora was the receptionist. **Nora was so enamored with this guy, she had no idea she had just helped him pull off the jewel heist of the decade. Her constant gossiping, whining and all-around whimpering was inexhaustible. Most bits and crumbs of gossip containing info on whereabouts and appointments were accurate. BUT!! The Breckenridge woman was not supposed to be home. She had frightened him as much as he did her. In fact, she had left the private clinic a day early from recovery. Johnny was not one to panic, but he did. He hit her and she went down. He did check her and did take the time to lay her on the bed, then got the hell out of there. Johnny Polo was not a thug. He was a good user and con, but not a thug.

He regained his composure, and quietly entered the waiting car as if he had just returned from a business meeting. Johnny motioned Conrad to drive on and instructed him where to drop him off. Johnny then handed Conrad the envelope for his services and said he would not be needing him anymore tonight. Everything went as smooth as silk, EXCEPT, damn it EXCEPT. Johnny didn't like it.

The woman and the jewels were high profile. Too much attention. Nora and her gossip about the Dr.'s clients had proven to be a double-edged sword for him. Johnny knew he could not stay in this town now, for too much longer. Best to move as quickly as possible. Nora was dumb, she knew nothing, but he was sure the police would be hot and heavy on everyone that had any contact at all with the Breckenridge woman. He had given Nora a token bracelet from the haul, simple and unassuming. The stones were small, the bracelet should not be a problem. Nora thought he was ready to pop the question that day.

He would hang around long enough to wine and dine her a few more times, say he had to go out of town on business for a while then get the hell out of here with no one the wiser. Just a couple more days Johnny, a couple more days, don't do anything to arouse suspicion. He cradled the jewels to his chest and thought irrationally about yachts, cracked crab, champagne, and lobster on sunset beaches. These were heady thoughts for an otherwise very careful and logical Johnny Polo.

Sorry Johnny, You are not the first Satan's Fire has consumed from avarice.

# Chapter 14

The demons were back. They had been dogging her for months now. At first, the visits were few and far between, then more frequently. She awoke in a cold sweat. She prayed for answers, hoping Harry was the answer to that prayer. Demons had not visited Maureen for a very long time. She thought she had buried them a long time ago.

The darkness did not come tonight on kitten feet. It fell harshly, and covered her in blackness and fear, as a red-faced hellion from the river Styx guided her through black waters torched with funnels of fire. Her legs were chained, and her body was drenched with beads of desperation and resignation. She screamed, no one heard, and the red-faced demon breathed his foul stink of death around her.

She awoke with a start as a hand reached out to her. It was Harry's. He was nothing but a dream, but she had to convince herself for a moment that he was not real. Her stirrings had alerted Max, who was quickly at her side, gently pawing her shoulder. A broad smile crossed her lips as the dog's concern for her, dissolved all specters of devils and demons. However, Maureen was finding the image of Mr. Harry Quinn was lingering in her thoughts just a little too long for comfort's sake.

As with Harry, love had eluded her. This was different from any thoughts of previous involvements. She always kept warm and friendly feelings for men in her life, but her brush with this man had a wow factor she had never experienced.

Absent-mindedly she opened the refrigerator and closed it just as fast. She filled a glass with ice and filled it with water.

"Come on Max, let's go to bed." That's all I need," she muttered to herself, bad dreams returning to keep scary premonitions and visions of my sister's intentions. The sisters' blood ran thick. Maureen had not had a night like this since she moved out of her uncle's house. With that she grabbed two Tylenol P.M. She knew there were bad days ahead.

She needed her sleep.

# Chapter 15

John summoned the family, and they all gathered in the great room of the house. Nora, Conrad, and Maureen had not seen each other since their aunt's funeral. Maureen had spoken to uncle John many times since then, but not her sister or brother, and she was not looking forward to socializing with them tonight. She brought Max along tonight to visit with Uncle John. The English springer spaniel had not seen him, since the loss of his wife. Man and dog greeted each other with love and affection.

John hugged the dog lovingly around the neck, happily accepting all pawing and whimpering sounds of "Hello". "Good to see you boy" The happiness of seeing his old master resounded as John stroked his head and back. In truth, Max was Diane's dog. His wife's death had affected John's life so profoundly, that he immersed himself in work, spending long hours at the office, and sometimes spending nights.

Maureen no longer found it a pleasure to come home from work after her aunt's death. The warmth was no longer there, and with her uncle fighting depression and spending long hours at work, Maureen decided to move. Max was miserable and unresponsive, the dog gave Nora and Conrad a wide berth, and there seemed to be no love lost on their side either, as indicated by their treatment of the animal.

And so, it was that Maureen moved, she could not bear to leave Max with the likes of her sister and brother, and when she closed the door behind her on moving day, Max happily went with her, and uncle John thought it best for all concerned.

The reunion between man and dog was interrupted when the front doorbell rang. Harry was indeed prompt, and John answered quickly, and immediately led with introductions to his children, Maureen, Conrad, and Nora. And this is Max.   The dog, hearing his name, extended a paw to Harry, who immediately recognized him as the dog in the oil painting behind John's desk.

Introductions were brief but long enough for Harry to have his notorious detective instincts kick in. The brother Conrad had already made a hasty but accurate decision. Worthless, self-absorbed, and materialistic immediately came to mind. But the sister Nora, he was taken aback. She was the mirror image of Maureen. But this woman was icy cold and calculating. Her image and burning gaze were disconcerting, and the touch of her hand on introduction revealed a woman of secrets and deceit. She looked like Maureen, but that's where it ended.

Sinister was the word that leaped to Harry's decisive appraisal. Nora reeked of it. There was no softness. Her eyes were piercing, malevolent, like a cobra. Harry all but shuddered openly when he shook her hand, again marveling at the polar feelings he felt from the twins.

He regained his composure, and, of course, said something charming about beauty coming in double doses in John's household.

"Shall we all get to it?"

"Your Uncle feels he needs more security at his warehouse, home, and office. and he has chosen our company to provide security for any new or innovative things that may be coming out. My presentation will be short, the system is not that difficult, but he did want all the family to know the coding, and how the system works. Should the system be triggered by accident, there is a simple code and procedure in shutting it down."

Harry continued his demonstration of the system, as the family all listened attentively. However, Nora's interest seemed clearly more intense than brother Conrad's. Her eyes hungrily followed Harry, indicating to him that she was far more interested in something other than his silly speech. The woman was consuming him with her eyes. He was being judged like a prize bull at a county fair. It was humiliating and demeaning. Two human feelings Harry Quinn rarely felt in his life.

Harry quickly wrapped the demo up, and Conrad quickly dismissed himself and was gone. Maureen and John politely asked if Harry would like a refreshment, to which Harry declined, thanked them, and would be on his way.

As Harry beat a hasty retreat, Nora quickly took him by the arm as she escorted him to the door. Her good-bye was lingering, as her eyes bored into his. She again extended her hand to his, her touch evoking in him an almost discernable disgust. Harry had never encountered a human being that elicited from him such powerful black emotion. It was then he noticed the fiery reflection from a stone on her bracelet that broke this woman's spell. He thanked Nora for her time and assured her if she has any questions her uncle has his number

# Chapter 16

Harry could not help himself. He found himself pulling up in front of her apartment. Calling her from the street, he hoped she hadn't eaten yet, and did everything but invite himself up to see her. He came bearing hot pizza and cold beer. How could she refuse? Joe, the apartment concierge, reluctantly smiled as Harry ushered his way into the elevator.

Seeing her greet him at the door and invite him in seemed as natural as his coming home. Max was also there to greet this newcomer. A newcomer, he seemed to completely approve of. The fact that he brought pizza didn't seem to hurt the new relationship either.

"Let's see," Harry offered. "If I remember, it was sausage, bacon, hamburger, mushroom, and peppers, on thin crust, the works, am I right?"

"You do remember." she chuckled, as she motioned to the coffee table and remote for the nightly news.

Harry popped the brews for them, turned on the news, and sat comfortably down, waiting for her to join him. This was the first time Harry had been in her apartment, but he felt a comfort level with her and her surroundings that made him all warm and secure inside, far removed from his experience earlier today with her family. It was not like Harry to make himself at home, and familiar so quickly, especially with a client.

Like two kids they sat together eating and drinking, having a light conversation, both seemingly trying to avoid any mention of Maureen's sister. It was Harry who first spoke of the family gathering. He did not disguise his true feelings about his first impression of Nora to Maureen when she prompted his response to her sister. Harry did not understand the visionary and psycho stuff Maureen experienced, but he did feel that her sister was capable of anything. He could at least believe the horrible visions that Maureen was living with were somehow tied to her sister, Nora, and his impression that this woman was a dedicated sociopath.

Harry believed Maureen, but the question remained, how do you prove and prevent a murder that hasn't happened! He could only imagine the torment she was going through. Harry turned to her in frustration, not knowing exactly what to do, but assured her he would stay close to John.

Realizing this man truly understood, and knew the burden she was carrying alone, she broke down. Maureen completely opened up to him and revealed all the sleepless nights, filled with nightmares she was having since her sister's return. The night-terrors were increasing, becoming far more vivid and real. Something was going to happen, and soon. Her confession left her visibly shaken and spent.

Harry pulled her to him. Holding her close, she nestled down in the crook of his arm while Harry, like a lullaby, in soft cooing tones, softly bid her sleep.

# Chapter 17

Nora pondered the events of the day. She was not happy. She had not heard from Johnny Polo in over a week and the situation around her uncle's business and home were changing.  Her uncle seemed to be taking a renewed interest in the business and was tightening his grip on the poorly managed projects left to his employees to figure out. He was un-attentive to his staff, some who had been with him for years, and left them at sea unable to make decisions, to move things forward. Nora had not envisioned her Uncle's depression to abate. She had planned so carefully, she became attentive to his every need, sympathetic and helpful. She fostered his depression, approving of his reclusive ways, and dependence on her to step in with worrisome employees, and household needs. He had allowed her a small inroad to the checkbook.

She made decisions on maintenance on the house, grounds, and groceries, but that is where it ended. John would not relinquish his complete control, but he always would share with her any thought he might have regarding the home or company. It was still his approval and signature that gave a final blessing to any large decision associated with his wealth and business. Nora had not broken that barrier yet.

SOMETHING WAS WRONG! The power spoke inside her. Everything was going so beautifully! She knew nothing about this! John did not say a word to her about this development, or that gorgeous insurance guy popping up giving directions. She felt the power decreasing. Failure of the second marriage had driven Nora back home.

In lieu of another husband on the horizon, Nora hatched other plans to secure her future. She would not have them upset. Nora had gone to extreme lengths for that cause. Removal of uncle John's wife had first become her objective. Diane had become a nuisance. She was too much the center of uncle John's universe. Nora was sick of her sweet ways and constant do-gooder attitude. Diane would appeal to Nora for her involvement in charitable affairs, and happily invite her to participate in her hobbies and club functions. Diane was a woman of substance and respect, she was loved by everyone. Nora could not stand her, or her dog.

And that garden, and those damnable flowers, how appropriate she should meet her demise in her blooming paradise by a pair of large copperheads placed appropriately in her cherished azaleas. Poor Diane, she and her weak heart would never survive this freak attack. The thought of this accident so perfectly executed, with the dog barking frantically in the background brought pure pleasure to the performance in the form of a wicked grin. Snakes were always her favorite.

This delicious thought evaporated quickly, as she continued to fret over this new set of circumstances she encountered this evening. And what had Maureen to do with this? She hadn't been around in months. Nora had wanted her gone too, it couldn't have worked out better. Maureen had the "Gift" also, but never engaged in it. Troubling thoughts plagued Nora's resolve. It was not good having Maureen around. She would talk to Uncle John tomorrow about how wise it was for him to install these security measures. It was best for the family and the business. She would also ask for the name of the man who demonstrated it, should she have any concerns or questions regarding the surveillance system.

Her sister's being there, and the timing of this installation unbeknownst to her continued to plague her until her cell phone interrupted her thoughts.

It was Johnny Polo. Her dangerous dark mood lifted. It was about time.

# Chapter 18

Two perfectly in-tuned bodies stirred sleepily and softly as the morning crept slowly through shuttered windows. The soft rays of the sun fell like silk upon her face, as she again nestled deep into his chest. Sleep was retreating slowly this morning. It was not until she heard this faraway comforting voice say "good morning" did she awake. Maureen had not felt the cloak of night and its peaceful sleep for weeks. She lingered there momentarily, then came to full attention. "Hello" "Have you been here all night?"

"Well, hello to you too." Now she was embarrassingly awake. "I'm so sorry"

"For what?" "Max and I caught up on some serious movie watching. Aaaa, may I use your facilities?" he asked as he rose from an obviously cramped position.

"Oh yes, yes of course." Maureen reached out to help straighten him up. "Would you like some coffee?"

His response was a big "Yes, Definitely, Black. Just as soon as I get the blood back in my arm." He responded to her with a big smile. She grinned back at him sheepishly and rushed to the kitchen.

His coffee was hot, black, and steaming on the counter, waiting for him as he emerged from the other room. She had quickly cleaned up the remains of their "Pizza party" from last night, tidied up, and was putting a jacket on with a leash in her hand. Harry's look begged a response,

"Oh, it's Saturday, Max's day," as she hooked up his leash.

"Hey wait a minute, Max and I both could use a walk." He took two big chugs of coffee and winced.

"Oh alright, you can come, but let me get you a go-cup."

Pouring the coffee into her thermos cup, the three hit the lobby with a cheery hello from Joe to Ms. Brady. "Same to you Joe," Maureen acknowledged as Max pulled her along for his overdue relief.

The fall season was in full array and the air was light and invigorating. Max knew the routine, and as he pulled the two forward, the definite sound of a sportscar drew close to the building.

Conrad noticed the two walking toward the small little park area at the end of the street. Questions buzzed in his head. Nora had called last night insisting he "visit" his sister. She wanted to know why and what the hell she was doing at the house last night, and why John felt she needed to know the workings of this new system. Nora had not heard from Maureen in months. Conrad was not at all curious, but now, as he watched the two walking, he immediately recognized Harry as the insurance man who his uncle had at the house yesterday. This was an unusual turn of events, so he did not hang around.

Nora insisted he drop in to say hello and to see how many contacts Maureen was having with her uncle John. Maureen had this sickening habit of checking in with her family periodically. She did it with Nora until Nora made it perfectly clear she did not like to be "smothered" and Uncle John did not need to be bothered. He was having a difficult time adjusting to Diane's death. He needed quiet for the healing process. Nora definitely did not want her around. Nora's unique instincts kicked in.

Conrad needed money and when he came to her for money, (she didn't have it) she insisted he ask Maureen for it. It certainly would be plausible for Conrad's visit. He had "borrowed" money from her many times before. These fractured thoughts about Maureen came to an end when Conrad's car pulled up under the arched driveway. On his announcement that he didn't talk to Maureen this morning but saw the "insurance guy" at Maureen's walking the dog this morning, Nora's agitated demeanor turned deadly.

# Chapter 19

Harry tagged happily along as Maureen and Max hit a moderate pace to the small green zone at the end of the street. He was a contented man this morning with a smile on his face. Spending the evening with her seemed to banish any pressing matters he needed to attend to. He just wanted to be with her. They sat down on a nearby bench after a brief jog.

The morning was crisp, and the day was clear and blue. Maureen threw her face to the morning sun, closing her eyes to enjoy its warmth when she felt his eyes upon her.

"What is this?" She grinned broadly as she turned to him.

"Oh nothing", he grinned just as broadly back at her. "I just like seeing you relax, and sleep," he added.

"Oh", she blushed. "Again, I apologize for that. I can't tell you how long it has been since I slept with such abandon and freedom."

"I would do it again in a heartbeat." he countered."

"That Mr. Quinn, I'm sure would get very old, very quickly."

"Never, MiLady, even if you do snore."

"If that's your idea of chivalry, I'll pass. Come on, the least I can do is make you breakfast. And I don't snore."

"Whatever you say. I won't take a chance on blowing a good breakfast."  "Come on Max." The dog was lying quietly at their feet, enjoying Maureen's new friend.

As the threesome entered the building, Harry thought he might have won Max's approval. However, he was not so sure about Joe, the apartment concierge, who eyed him suspiciously as he escorted Max and Maureen into the elevator.

"If you need anything, Ms. Brady," he called after her, you just give me a call."

"Thanks, Joe."

Maureen looked at Harry appraisingly, up and down. "You may or may not have passed inspection"

"Umm, did I or didn't I"

"I don't know, I'll let you know."

They exited the elevator in a myriad of giggles.

Springtime had come early for Maureen Brady and Harry Quinn.

# Chapter 20

Johnny Polo was packing as he sweet-talked Nora. Women are so stupid, he thought as he purred into the phone, telling her how much he was sorry business would be taking most of his time this next two weeks. He had planned a romantic dinner and send-off that night to tell her how much he loved her, and would miss her. He could hear her practically drooling through the phone. The older ones were always an easier mark. After tonight Johnny Polo would be gone to parts unknown, thinking he had pulled off the greatest con of all time. He would be glad to leave this woman behind. There was something almost scary about her, but worth every minute invested in her. Time was not on his side.

The jewels were too hot. Any association with the theft was remote, very remote, but knowing the cops, there would be questions for everyone. The butcher, the baker, the candlestick maker, the plastic surgeon, his receptionist, etc., etc., anyone Breckenridge had contact with. Nora knew nothing, but he couldn't take any chances. Johnny Polo was going to see that she had a beautiful evening, with more to come on his return. At least a return she will be looking forward to that will never happen.

# Chapter 21

Harry reluctantly left Maureen's apartment about noon. Reality set in and Harry realized he hadn't thought of anything but Maureen and being with her. He was lost in her presence for the last 24 hours and had not checked in the office. Tiffany would be worried, it was not like him. He called, put her mind at ease, and suffered a well-deserved scolding. She also reminded him of the files remaining on his desk, and the calls he needed to return, nothing serious, but Josh called yesterday afternoon and said he would be in the office for a while on Saturday.

When the elevator door opened, Harry was greeted by Joe the "gatekeeper's" disapproving gaze. Understanding, Harry turned to him, walked over to his security perch, and took the time to assure him that he was on his best behavior. He also enlisted Joe's help by asking him to contact him if he saw anything, or anyone out of the ordinary, or suspicious, to him, where Miss Brady was concerned. With that, he handed him his card and told him to call anytime. "I assure you, we both have her best interest at heart."

Once convinced Harry was an OK guy, Joe smiled broadly, and said he would keep an eye out, and if Ms. Brady needed anything just let him know. Harry offered a stipend to Joe for his help, but Joe would have none of it. Almost offended by Harry's offer, Joe quickly shot back that he would do that anyway,

"Miss Maureen is good people."

"Thanks, Joe, have a good day."

It was Saturday, his building was mostly quiet, and he entered his office with the best of intentions for work. He could not shake his thoughts of Maureen and her concern for her uncle, and her nagging night terrors.

He called Josh, not as a business associate, but as a friend. He unloaded. His feelings for Maureen, and his helplessness in his ability to help her.

This was a rare confession for Harry Quinn, an independent, controlled, self-contained tough-guy detective. Josh had never experienced this side of the man. He listened attentively, and reminded Harry, in all the years he and his father knew him, there was nothing that Harry would walk away from or could not figure out an answer for. As far as love is concerned that is something no one has the answer for. You have to figure that one out yourself.

When the man-to-man talk ceased, Josh casually asked if he had a chance to look at the files he gave him.

Harry was staring down at them as they spoke. "I'll get to it right now. I'll call you."

He cleared his head, picked up the manila file, and rifled through the paperwork. He studied the police and medical report, photos of the victim, the home, surroundings, and crime scene. The police did not have a clue or a lead. The Insurance company had every jewelry piece categorized. Its type of setting, and value. Harry memorized the photo of every ring, brooch, necklace, and bracelet.

This was far too big a haul for someone not to have heard of it out on the street. He reviewed it again, saw Mrs. Breckenridge's statement, and saw that she was recovering nicely on an added update. He would interview Mrs. Breckenridge Monday if she was up to it, and get the word out to his people on the street. This would be a beautiful recovery fee. If the insurance snoops didn't get there first.

"Satan's fire" worth millions, Harry marveled at the value of each piece. Then his eyes fell on a piece that resurrected a small green flash in his memory. He casually disregarded it as one of those deja vu things. He called Mrs. Breckenridge, introduced himself and his interest in the recent theft of her jewels. Harry explained that over the years he had worked free-lance with the police and insurance companies, with thefts of this magnitude, Mrs. Breckenridge was more than happy to see him, she just wanted her emeralds back, and the person responsible to be caught.

Any loose ends that Tiffany had asked him about, he took care of, called John to see if all was well, and again reminded him to stay alert, be cautious of his surroundings, and call him if anything is out of the ordinary in his day. He then called Maureen, he could not let the rest of the day go by without speaking to her. He told her he had just spoken to her uncle, and things were well with him.

"I'm glad you checked on him. I was just about to call him myself. Now I know there are two of us looking out for him."

"I know I liked watching over his niece last night."

"It was a lovely evening," she responded.

Harry quickly volunteered to repeat her sleep routine from last night, if she needed a dreamcatcher, but she politely declined with a soft chuckle, telling him his reassurance would help her sleep tonight. Reluctantly he said goodbye, he would call her tomorrow. He left the office and decided he was hungry. He had not eaten since their breakfast this morning. He stopped for Chinese take-out.

# Chapter 21

Nora lay back in delusional splendor. She had just taken Johnny Polo to the airport and put him on the red-eye to Philadelphia. She found herself far too excited to go to work. She called and left a message that she would not be in Monday. Johnny had shown her such a beautiful evening last night. He was surprisingly sweet and attentive, taking her to the finest hotel and restaurant, and ending their evening with Nicolas Feuillatte champagne and red roses, at their bedside. He apologized for his work distracting him at times but assured her that after this merger, life would be better for both of them. Having to put him on that flight, after their special evening of lovemaking, and whispers of their future together, was like denying a child her favorite toy. She couldn't bear the separation but amused herself for the moment by thinking of the events of the previous evening until her fantasies lulled her to sleep.

For a woman of considerable intelligence, a shrewd and calculating mind, and above all, a completely self-absorbed human being, Nora found herself completely mesmerized with this man. When she awoke, she spent the rest of the day in childlike wonderment. Per Johnny's instructions, she started planning a small intimate wedding and devoured dozens of travel brochures in warm sunny climes for the perfect honeymoon retreat. She couldn't wait to hear from Johnny to share.

He called later that evening to tell her he had landed, and couldn't wait to get back to her asap. What he didn't tell her was that it wasn't Philadelphia where he landed, it was Bermuda, and he had left the airport with passport and ID as Thomas Conman. Ohhh, that Johnny Polo was very, very, good. As he disembarked from the plane into the sunny climes of Bermuda, a red mustang convertible driven by a dark haired beauty with exotic eyes picked him up. She was 23, and wore a stunning pair of EMERALD earrings.

# Chapter 22

Harry's Sunday activities were usually a day of rest and review of the previous week. Sometimes a game of golf, poker, football, a good book, or classic old movies. Reluctantly he would work out 2-3 times a week, Sunday usually being one of them.

He had brought the Breckenridge file home with him, reviewed it again, but found his mind wandering to the lady Maureen. Defeated and distracted, he called Maureen to see if she and Max needed a mid-day walk and would she meet him for what he promised to be the "best chili dog in the country, a true culinary experience.  With callous abandon and the promise of a busy week ahead for her, she disregarded the favorite book of the month club and promptly accepted the "best chili dog in the world" invitation. How could she not?

"Pick you up in an hour?"

"Max and I will be downstairs waiting."

Max greeted Harry with a wag of the tail and a slight "I'm happy to see you bark" as Harry held the door open for him. Max fit nicely in the back of the big BMW, just like he belonged there. The two, man and beast seemed to form an immediate connection, a fact that did not go unnoticed by Maureen. She believed in the instincts of animals.

"Fasten your seatbelt, you are in for a treat"

"This better be good"

"Trust me."

And she did. Just a short drive out of town they stopped at a designated park and animal sanctuary with biking and walking trails. The day was beautiful, bright and brisk, filled with activity, with many catching the last throes of autumn before winter set in. Max took over the driving, or rather navigating from Harry, as he found a new place to explore. There was no doubt who was taking who, where. When Max had exhausted his exploratory nature, the dog let Harry have control. Over the next hill, Harry was about to fulfill his promise.

The unmistakable smell of hot dogs slowly came wafting through the air. A large red umbrella-covered a man dressed in butcher garb and apron. He wore the consummate chef's hat and had a huge black mustache. It was too delicious and obvious not to notice. He was the perfect chef. His stainless-steel vendor's wagon was immaculate. And all the many choices of condiments were neatly stationed. His chili was homemade and several of his cheeses were imported. Harry ordered three. Max would have his plain. Maureen asked Harry to please choose for her, he had done such a good job so far on the day. She and Max would be waiting by a nearby picnic table.

"I hope you like onions," whispering in her ear, as he set the exquisite dogs before them.

"I do."

When all evidence of hot dogs was gone, the burning question remained.

"Was it or wasn't it?" Harry looked on in rapt anticipation.

"YES, YES," she cried, "you win."

The laughter between the two ricocheted throughout the trees.

This was not a wasted day of abandonment or filling of the day with frivolous words between two people. This day set the stage and wrote the pages for the rest of their lives.

# Chapter 23

Harry walked her to the door about 5:00 that afternoon and reluctantly left her at the elevator. They both agreed, they had a wonderful afternoon and would do it again soon. They spoke of her uncle and approval of the new security system, it helped to relax her fears a little about his well-being.

Maureen had been sleeping better, the restless sleep and nightmares had all but stopped the last few days, and the horrible visions had ceased.

"I know this must be hard for you to understand, but these thoughts and feelings I have are very real. I've lived with them since I was a young girl."

These words said to him would have been very true, had he not lived through the winter of two years ago when he experienced the exorcism of a true demon. There is a dark side to this life.

Harry had become a believer in such things since his friends removed such a curse from their home. Their lives were in mortal danger. Harry became a full-fledged member of the Other Worldly Club. He assured Maureen that he indeed did not understand the feelings, but he did know about the existence of evil, and some peoples' ability to know when it was at work. Harry kissed her on the cheek, saw her and Max into the elevator, and said he would check in with John tomorrow morning.

As he approached the door to leave, he heard a voice call out to him. It was Joe. He was not at his station when they arrived. Harry turned to greet him and was met by the anxious concern of Joe's protective instincts for Maureen.

"Hey, Mr. Quinn, someone stopped by here today who was the mirror image of Miss Maureen. I couldn't believe what I was looking at, and said she was looking for her sister. I didn't even know Miss Maureen had a sister. I left her a message   to get in touch with her, but I thought you would like to know."

"Yes, yes I would Joe. Thanks for telling me."

With news of Maureen's sister turning up at her door, the once contented face of Harry Quinn only minutes ago turned dark and brooding.

"That woman, Mr. Quinn," Joe had one more parting observation, "that woman is bad news Mr. Quinn, really bad news. As if, he thought for a moment, "Malevolent". "That's it, Grimm's fairy tale stuff. Don't ask me how I know, I just know. You take care of yourself, Mr. Quinn."

"Thanks, Joe. I'll try my best," knowing just exactly what Joe was talking about.

A chill ran down his spine, as he walked out the door. His intuition told him he would be hearing from the wicked witch very soon.

# Chapter 24

Johnny Polo stretched languidly beneath the brightly colored umbrella of his cabana, with a drink in hand and alone with his thoughts, he reflected on the events of the past month and his good fortune. The beach was quiet, and the soft whisper of the surf allowed him to conjecture where he might be next month. He could go anywhere and do anything he wanted to do. After all Johnny Polo had just graduated from two-bit hustler to international cat burglar. A wide grin, showcasing his perfect white teeth couldn't help hide his good fortune. And to think he almost walked away from that one.

Johnny had just spoken to Nora about an hour ago telling her how hard he was working and was looking forward to getting home to her next week. His feigned interest in her, and her day, opened a whole deluge of complaints and mundane offerings about her work and uncle, however, he did note that through that whole discourse of the weeks happening, she did mention that the police had stopped by her office regarding that assault on Mrs. Breckenridge to interview her doctor, and talk to a couple of the nurses, and then continue on with her outpourings of how shabby the world was treating her and she couldn't wait till he returned and so on and so on. Johnny had found out what he wanted to know. He was glad he got out when he did.

"Now, now, just hold on baby, I'll be back before you know it, and we'll go out and celebrate."

Nora cooed back to the charming Johnny Polo, professing her undying love. "Keep thinking where we're going to spend our honeymoon Baby Doll, and I'll be home before you know it". Nora loved it when he called her Baby Doll.

With a giant sigh of relief, he removed himself from her tedious harangue, vowing only a couple of more calls to her, and Johnny Polo would be out of her life forever. Nora didn't have a clue that Johnny had anything to do with the Breckenridge heist. He was happy he learned from Nora's ramblings that the old woman Breckenridge was recovering. After all, he had a lot to be grateful for from her. Johnny Polo may be a heartbreaker, but he was not a thug, no sir.

Content there was no connection between him and Breckenridge, he rode his senses on the incoming breezes of the Mediterranean to the high mountain passes of Switzerland, only to be interrupted by a girl from Ipanema type sauntering down the beach in the late afternoon sun. Ummm….Life was good!

# Chapter 25

This other person Nora had become was quite remarkable. It was as if Nora had left her devious, vicious self, tied up in a closet. This was a woman of thirty-six, twice married who was acting like an empty-headed schoolgirl, and empty-headed is something Nora Bradford was not. This man Johnny had infected her. Her calculating and murderous plans for her uncle had been side-tracked and she had all but forgotten her busybody sister Maureen was becoming all too chummy with him since she moved out. Since Johnny came into her life, she thought little of her loser brother and the rest of the family. There was no love lost for any of them. Nora was tired of them all, and when Johnny got back, they would be gone forever.

Her cell interrupted her idyllic reveries, and she answered to her sister's inquiry on the other end.

"Hi sis, I hear you're looking for me?"

"Well yes, I did drop by and found you were not home. I thought we could meet for lunch, catch up on things, and you can tell me if Uncle John talked to you about updating his insurance on the business and home with the camera alarm system. Frankly, I was surprised to see you there."

"Well yes, I know you're the one who helps with some of the everyday business issues, but Uncle John felt with you working now, he wanted me to know a little of what was happening. But yes, we could meet for lunch and catch up on things. I understand you have a new guy."

"Who told you that?"

"Oh, Conrad might have mentioned he thought you might have a new beau. You'll have to tell me all about him. Why don't you ask Conrad if he'd like to come along?"

"I think I'll just meet you solo for some girl talk. How about we make it Tuesday at 12:00? I've got Tuesday off this week. I think this temp job is just about over for me."

When Nora said goodbye to Maureen, she found that talking to her sister left her in an extremely bad mood. With less than an hour from talking to

Johnny, she found herself calling him back. He did not answer. Nora got his voicemail four times. On the fourth try, an old beast stirred within her. Nora was angry.

# Chapter 26

Harry phoned Maureen at her office in the morning, first to check in on her, and secondly to remind her that his gourmet hot dog that weekend was made twice as satisfying with her as his company. The warmth of her response to their weekend brought a smile of satisfaction to his lips. He inquired as to how she was feeling, and if she was having any more nightmares or visions, hoping to hear a positive response from her.

Maureen had been sleeping better and she, like Harry, wanted this all to go away. She had cautioned Harry that lately, these visions had become more active. This was the deciding factor that drove her to seek help from him in the first place. This past week they seem to have gone in remission, but she was not confident at all that they were gone for good. She was not ready to abandon her concerns for her Uncle.

Harry understood, and said he was driving out to check on him today. He had called earlier to find him at home, and John agreed to see him early this afternoon at the house.

"I'm glad you're going to see him. I would like to think these issues would all resolve themselves, and I wouldn't feel he needed protection, but for now, my instincts tell me otherwise. I also heard from Nora. Joe told me she stopped by to see me. We're having lunch tomorrow to catch up."

"I know, Joe also told me you had a visitor. His opinion of her was not very flattering, between you and me of course."

"She can have that effect on people."

"You have a good day, and I'll talk to you soon."

John greeted Harry at the door with an enthusiastic hello.

"Come on in, Harry, it's good to see you."

"Good to see you too John. Just thought I would come by and check on you. Everything ok?"

"You know Harry, it is. Regardless of the reasons you contacted me, it was good that I upgraded everything. It made me realize just how much I had been neglecting the business since Diane's death. Grief can be a debilitating thing. She would never allow me to feel sorry for myself or to remain in a state of limbo.  I've been going to the office but just been going through the motions, spending time there because I just did not want to come home. I've tried to stay close to the family, but have been unable to. Actually for the past few years. I feel I've turned a corner, and am looking forward to a new project we're working on down at the plant."

"That's good to hear John, you look like you feel better, you've been getting some sun. Look, has there been anything unusual or suspicious John?"

"No, no can't say that there has been, but you're coming here, and me finding that camera in my office has made me far more alert to things than I have been in a year. But I can't say anything is out of the ordinary."

"That's good to know. Caution is still the operative word here. This whole thing may prove to be nothing but an overactive imagination or bad intel, but until we're sure, just carry on as you always have. You, uh, still can't say who hired you?"

"I'm sorry John, I know it sounds crazy to you. Hell, I'll say it again it sounds crazy to me, yet here

I am. I'm being paid for someone's concern for you. And no, I can't tell you who it is and no you can't tell anyone around you."

The door to John's office opened. Nora was home early.

"Oh, I'm sorry Uncle John, I didn't mean to interrupt."

"Come in Nora, you remember Mr. Quinn? He came by to check on our new system."

"Of course, I do. Hello again," and extended her hand.

Harry reluctantly rose to the occasion and shook her hand. The woman gave him the willies. He couldn't believe he was staring into a carbon copy of Maureen. This woman was not the woman that turned his life inside out. She was the opposite of all things good and beautiful in Maureen. He tried as before to release his hand from her lingering grasp.

"So nice to see you again Ms. Bradford."

"I just came in to check the books Uncle John and receivables,"

"Don't worry about those Nora, they're done."

"I've been taking up enough of your time."

"Well, we were just about done here, John I'll be on my way, I have another appointment, keep in touch."

"Well if that's the case," Nora chimed in, "I'll just show Harry to his car."

Without hesitation, Harry found himself firmly in an armlock with Ms. Bradford, who suddenly had lost all memory of how the alarm system worked, and would he be so kind as to show her the procedure again. Trapped, dutifully Harry took her to the control box and pointed out all cameras, lights and the code system, emergency numbers, and false alarm shut-downs. She would have to put her passcode in of course as he proceeded with his demonstration, and as her fingers brushed his hand to touch the keyboard, the alarms went off. But it was not in the system, it was the intuitive memory of Harry's mind. Nora's wrist displayed the "one of a kind" emerald bracelet Harry had committed to memory from the insurance file on "Satan's Fire." Time stood still for a brief second. Harry regained his composure and found his interest in Nora was now more than a reason for a quick exit. He immediately turned on his most charming and chivalrous self. Taking Nora by the hand, he assured her that he would be more than happy to answer any more questions she may have about the system and he would be completely at her disposal should she need any more guidance. With a slight titter, she thanked him, and arm-in-arm she walked him to his car and thanked him again for his tolerance of her ineptness.

Basking in her performance, remembering she had played the lead in Antony and Cleopatra, she waved to him as the BMW fell into the distance.

Harry, who endured the performance as an audience of one would have surely critiqued the lead player as not Cleopatra, but the asp.

# Chapter 27

It was early when he called. "I'm sorry baby," Johnny breathed into the phone, I misplaced my phone. I was hoping someone would turn it in, but no such luck. Look, you got the new number on your phone now?"

"Yes, yes Johnny, I have it."

Johnny was notorious for losing his phone, this was the second one, or was it the third one in six months she had known him, that he had lost.

"I'm much better now, I know you're alright."

"Will you be home soon?"

"Couple more meetings, and issues to be ironed out, but I should be home by this weekend,"

"Everything ok on your end?"

"Well you know Johnny, nothing is ever ok when you're not here. Hey, how is the job, still have the police hanging around your office? At least you have some excitement going on."

"I would not call my receptionist job exciting, but no they haven't been. Mrs. Breckenridge came in for her follow-up, and we heard all about it. She seems fine, can't seem to remember a thing about the thief. She knows she caught him by surprise, and she's just grateful to be alive.  But no one has a clue about anything. She's beside herself about the theft. It's still all over the news, but she looks great! Amazing what money can do!"

"Look I have to go, Baby Doll. Talk to you tonight."

So far, so good. It was dumb luck that got him this far. He didn't want to make any mistakes now. He showered and shaved, bought a used car from a local to avoid rental agencies, and did some island hopping.

Johnny Polo had been here long enough.

# Chapter 28

arry sat deep in thought, studying the file before him. that Josh had given him the file last week regarding the Satan's Fire collection. He stared down at the pictured bracelet with its unique scrolling and dragon heads. He would have to check to be sure, but he was almost positive this was the bracelet he saw on Nora, right down to its unique clasp with two small emeralds in the face of a Chinese dog. He was confused and torn. Everyone was suspect now, Maureen, her sister, even John, and the brother. He had to find out if this, indeed, was the same bracelet. The only person he could confide in at this point was Josh.

It was late, but Harry felt this couldn't wait. He called Josh and caught him at home. "Look, Josh, I'm telling you what I think I saw. You did tell me these pieces were all one of a kind, no copies that you know of?"

"That's what I've been told. If what you say is true, Harry, every insurance investigator will be beating down your door. This is still red hot. You read the provenance on several of the pieces?"

"Well, I don't want to jump the gun. I'm going to try and see the piece again.  It means getting closer to Maureen's sister. You know, Josh, the one I'm crazy about. I can't trust her or her family until I know what's going on. I just thought you should know. Josh, I'd like to keep this under wraps for the time being."

"Understood."

"I'll call you when I know more." With that done, he called Maureen. He missed her, and wanted to hear from her and ask all the mundane questions, like how was your day, did you have a good dinner, and did you sleep well, just to hear her talk to him. He silently prayed she was not involved in this, she couldn't be.

When she answered with that soft silky voice of hers, he found himself hesitating, like a schoolboy in response. No, he would not believe it. But in the course of their conversation, he said nothing regarding the bracelet. He did say he thought he should get to know her sister better. She had become very interested in how the security system worked and he was going to offer to take her for a cup of coffee. Why Maureen felt the need to say be careful to him, he did not know, but she did say her nights were becoming more restless and bits and pieces of bad dreams came calling. He promised he would be careful.

He had to get a better look at that bracelet.

# Chapter 29

As Harry opened the door for Nora in his most courtly manner, he checked her arm to see that she was wearing the bracelet. Relieved, he saw she had added several more baubles to enhance her fashion statement. She had left work early to get the complete makeover for her gentlemen caller tonight. The use of one of two credit cards balked at the additional financial burden she added to it, but she felt this man was certainly worth the extra effort.

She would not germinate at home waiting for Johnny to call. She had left two more messages for him, and he had failed to respond. Attention from Harry tonight would relieve her of terrible thoughts about Johnny. He had no business ignoring her like this. Besides, she found Johnny to be nothing more than a slight distraction at the moment as she turned her attention to Harry.

"I thought we would dine at Rembrandt's tonight. I hope you like fine Italian. If you prefer, we can choose to go elsewhere."

Nora knew of the place and knew it to be popular, high dollar and the food excellent. It had made a reputation for itself in the past two years it had been opened. Immediately she approved. Gushing she thought he had made an excellent choice. This small exchange had prompted Harry to inquire about her likes and dislikes of particular foods, entertainment, and so on, for conversation's sake. Sadly, this small inquiry from him opened Pandora's box.

Words flowed from Nora's lips like a broken faucet. The conversation quickly turned from favorite foods to her lot in life, and how she had been treated by people. The unfairness of it all. She had bad breaks, no good affairs, terrible advice. Hates where she works, and the people she works for. Nora was a good talker. She whined about her family, her friends, the weather, and her uncle's house, and his lack of understanding. He smothered her, etc, etc, etc. Harry's mind went blank. All of life's miseries had taken up residence in a loft in a persecuted mind. Almost visibly unable to speak, Harry gladly turned the keys over to the valet at Rembrandt's.

This woman cannot have the same DNA as Maureen. Harry could not remember when he wanted an evening over so quickly. He escorted her in and was quickly ushered to his reserved table. Before allowing any long pre-chatter dinner talk, Harry quickly ordered the wine and entrée for both. Nora did not seem to mind. Reminding himself why he was here, his cavalier flattery reminded her again how lovely she looked in that dress, and noticed the beautiful bracelet she was wearing,

"May I?" he asked.

She quickly acquiesced, extended her arm, and he gently and reluctantly took her hand to examine it.

"My fiancée gave it to me."

"Oh well, he has very good taste."

"Yes, yes he does, but we won't worry about him tonight."

Thankfully, the waiter came with the entrée. It was unfortunate Harry could not enjoy his meal. He just wanted this night to be over, but he continued with the conversation gently probing about the boyfriend. Up to the second glass of wine, she was eager to give out particulars. But she seemed to tire of speaking about him tonight. Her interests were elsewhere, and Harry was determined to keep the conversation light and non-committal.

When it became obvious to him, she had no more interest in polite dining room banter, and rejected dessert, but would welcome an after-dinner drink, Harry became very concerned with the time. Nora had unleashed with laser-like precision unmistakable predatory female advances toward him, and he did not want to sever any budding relationship he had with her. So, he apologized profusely and begged to have her charming company at another time. He had an extremely busy day tomorrow that began quite early, and it was a bit of a drive to her place, besides he chuckled, "I told your Uncle I would have you home by ten."

He walked her to the door, told her he looked forward to their next meeting, said his goodnight, and left. She was completely charmed.

They did not talk about insurance or surveillance equipment.

# Chapter 30

"Josh, I have no doubt I was looking at the same bracelet pictured and numbered in the catalog. If you are sure it's one of a kind."

"Well nothing in this life is guaranteed, Harry. Even so, what are the odds? If you recover from this heist, you could retire for life."

"How does this all tie in with the sister Maureen you sent me last month. This all can't be a coincidence. Or can it? I'm telling you Josh these two women, twins or not, could not have come from the same mother." "I don't know what to tell you, Harry. Stranger things have happened, believe me, I know. Keep me posted. I have another call."

Josh no doubt was referring to an incident he experienced in Long Island last year in Ichabod Crane country. It was an incredible story Harry found almost impossible to believe, filled with devils, demons, and angels, but had to, because Josh Lawton was his friend, just as he had to believe that Maureen and her problem had nothing to do with the stolen jewels and the bracelet on her sister's arm. He needed to talk to her now, regardless. This missing bracelet could do nothing but introduce a shadow of suspicion on Maureen, something he must remember, when he spoke to her, no matter how painful. He called with mixed emotions.

"Hi, I thought we could meet for a quick cup of coffee, and I may be able to convince you to have dinner with me this weekend. I might even spring for more than a hotdog."

She could not help but smile when she heard his voice. "Sure, I would like that. I need to finish up here, should take me about twenty minutes. I'll meet you at the little café."

He was sitting in the rear, looking sullen as she walked in. As she walked toward him, all his tough guy, hard nose persona melted away when he saw her, and he knew with every gut instinct in him that Maureen could not be aligned or involved with her sister in any way but blood.

# Chapter 31

"How can you two be related" the words unforgivingly poured out of his mouth the minute she sat down.

"I get that a lot," she smiled. "I don't know how to answer that. We never were very close."

Harry closely looked at her, she seemed tired, and out of sorts. Little blue circles under her eyes stole the usual sparkle he saw in them.

"How are you sleeping?" His feelings for this woman were obviously making him far too defensive about her to be professional.

"Not very well the past two nights. How is Uncle John?"

"When I picked Nora up yesterday, he seemed to be quite well, as a matter of fact much better from the first time I saw him. He took me to the library, and we had a nice talk. Started to tell me a little about his wife. Then Nora came in and we left."

"Aunt Diane and Uncle John have really been my family. It was awful when we lost her. The whole household just kind of fell apart. I couldn't stand it around there anymore without her, and I left. Uncle John had a hard time coping around the house. Did he tell you how it happened?"

"Yes, very strange. How about you, why aren't you sleeping?"

I don't know. The nightmares are back. They are flickers. They are not coming in black and white anymore, it's like a kaleidoscope of colors in red and orange and black. I see the faces of my family falling, I'm unable to catch them, they disappear."

"Was Nora or Conrad in them?"

"Not that I can remember."

"Tell me what you can about Nora"

"Like I said, we were never close. When we were little, she and Conrad would have secrets. Technically I'm the older one. We were born in December. I remember my father telling me what a long and cold night it was. Snow was deep on the ground and a full moon filled the quiet night. It was a beautiful night. I came first, very quickly before midnight, Nora came afterward, and my mother had difficulty. It wasn't until the early morning of the twenty-second that she arrived. The weatherman said the next day it was unusual to have the full moon during the winter solstice. My mother said they almost named her Luna because of the beauty of the moon that night, but it came out Nora instead."

Maureen went on, "We had a great childhood, loving parents, but Nora and I just seemed to grow further and further apart. We had different likes and dislikes. She and Conrad got along far better. They always made me feel like I was an intruder, or interloper in their games. I would cry and complain to my mother they wouldn't let me play with them. And as we grew older, we just simply grew further and further apart. We never shared secrets, or talked about boys, or played sports. We both were pretty good students. I enjoyed history and English literature. I didn't care for math too much. Nora was better at it than me, but I never asked her for help. I seemed to be closer to our mother. We would shop together and cook and do projects for school together. Nora seemed to resent that. As a matter of fact, she was really quite the loner. I'm sorry Harry, I wish I could tell you more. After we lost our parents, it became even worse. We grew further apart, and I found myself uncomfortable around her, unable to trust or feel a closeness that sisters should have. Uncle John and Diane were a Godsend, I don't know what I would have done after losing our parents."

Maureen continued her story, "And Conrad, he just did what he could to finish school, and worked for Uncle John after college. I know that's not going too well. I think you know the rest of the story. I love the job I'm in. Nora married twice and left. I stayed here. Life was good. When Nora came back the second time, my whole well-being seemed to be affected, and I started having these premonitions, dreams whatever you want to call them. When we lost Diane, I just felt I couldn't stay here anymore. That's when the night terrors came back. So here we are, I'm not crazy, so that's when I talked to Josh for advice. Over the years, he has helped our family. He wasn't condescending, and he didn't laugh. He took me seriously and sent me to you. I'm scared something terrible is going to happen, and I feel helpless to prevent it."

He took her by the hand and tried to calm her, unsure himself of what to do. But more and more he felt Nora was the key to the misery of this family.

# Chapter 32

The words rang hollow, in short, impersonal staccato clips. "It will not be necessary for you to come in today Ms. Brady, we no longer are in need of your services. Your final paycheck and official letter will be sent to you. Thank you". The syrupy kiss-off voice was gone. Nora angrily threw the phone against the wall with such violence, it shattered into several pieces. She had lost another one. She needed money, and her uncle had ceased to pay her anything since his renewed interest in the business. In spite of the fact she lived in his beautiful home rent-free with all her comfort and needs provided for, it still was not enough. His benevolence grew thin. Nora was beside herself. Her anger mounted as she thought of Johnny. In spite of her many messages to him, she had not received a call from him in three days. His number went straight to voicemail, and finally, a recording echoing this is not a working number. The morning call from work and her dismissal revelation released a hate in her eclipsing the day she rid herself of her simpering parents.

The house was empty. Angrily she burst into her uncle's study and threw open the double doors to the garden. Running down the pathway, she called to her pets. Within minutes two very large undulating serpents collected at her feet. Lovingly she cooed to them. Whispering there was much to do in the coming days, begging them to be patient. As the serpents retreated, Nora cried out as a medieval fever engulfed her, a plague to her heart and soul. The Hate had been buried deep, like cancer in remission, came back with a vengeance. The beautiful features of her face became twisted and hardened, and an evil gripped her heart and soul. She called on The Evils of Old to remove all obstacles in her path, and prepare a torturous end to all that had wronged her. Nora had dismissed anything normal or human about her.

The unmasking felt good, it was liberating. She no longer needed a Johnny Polo to enrich her life. She did however need John, for the time being anyway. Maureen was disposable. And there was always a use for Conrad. The black power swelled within her, releasing all the alchemy of the dark places at her disposal. Exercising all the power and cruelty within her at the moment, she hesitated her defiant incantation. Nora reflected, she must keep a low profile, for the moment. Her now deformed face and twisted features with its waxy pallor and her knotty knuckled fingers must be hidden. The beautiful auburn hair had turned crusty, scaling wildly over her shoulders. Thoughts of Johnny Polo fueled the demon inside, preventing it from a hasty retreat. A shrieking voice escaped her mottled lips demanding all the fires of hell be visited upon him. The fury subsided. A foreboding calm took control. The mask of Nora was still needed. She must control herself. Even demons need time to predict and plan.

Johnny Polo, I don't envy you, wherever you are.

# Chapter 33

The soft tinkle of what seemed to be wind chimes caught John's ear at the open door of his study. It was pleasant and inviting, and he had no idea where it came from. For a moment he thought it was his imagination. He remembered Diane had hung one or two in the garden. He had not thought of that sound since her death. The sound was soothing, and he left the door open. It was not that cold, and the fresh air felt good. He had found the door slightly askew as he came in that morning with his coffee and paper. This was still his habit, regardless of the computer before him. He jealously guarded his alone time. The feel of a good book and a comfortable chair he found far more comforting than any new high-tech device. Diane had pulled him reluctantly into the brave new world of computerization. She had just converted the plant before their last vacation. He smiled as he thought of her.

His reverie was interrupted as Nora popped in asking if he needed anything or if he needed help with work from the office. John had told her no, and on several occasions. However, she had become increasingly cloying and worrisome about it. His solitude by then was broken. Insistent, she invited herself into his me time. John had found her to be increasingly more of a nuisance than a help.

She plopped herself down and announced to him her temp job had been terminated and she would have more time to help out with the books. John wished to God he had never allowed it to start. Courteous, as John always was, gently told her he was feeling much better now, and he felt it was not necessary for her to be involved.

Her persistence clung to his personal space. She asked him about the business, what new projects are going on, and how she missed going to the office and learning more about the family business. Her overzealous interest in the business was beginning to wear on him and he politely offered to speak of it over dinner tomorrow night, but for now, he was expecting a call. Reluctantly, Nora got the message.

She excused herself and offered to make his lunch a little later on, to which he declined. He definitely was not going to be here at lunchtime. Somehow, he felt he had just been through a police interrogation.

He went back to his paper, and his coffee, (which was now cold,) and tried to resume his pleasant morning. It didn't work.

# Chapter 34

The ancient one stirred. He had been awakened by the wind chimes carried on the soft winds. The old wolf rose and stretched. Evil was near. His journey would not be long. His presence in the face of evil was required. Centuries of instinct and callings of the universe had again reminded him of his purpose to combat evil and all its minions. He was not alone. Others throughout the universe had the calling.

The dark-hearted one from below came in many different forms, requiring the services of many to keep His dark shadow from covering the earth. Since the Dark One's banishment from the Heavens, Beelzebub has been sowing seeds of dissension throughout the land. The Great Master has chosen his damnation to be forever, for such was his sin that He must never be allowed a foothold on God's good earth again.

Over many eons, the Dark One and his fallen followers have attempted to regain power through deceit and trickery, bringing chaos and pain to the world. Sometimes a demon's chosen individual brings cruelty and discourse to all around them, and sometimes in such magnitudes as earthquake, flood, famine, and war. Evil came in all sizes, shapes, and disasters. It was a constant, destined to be overcome and conquered for an eternity. From the smallest unkind word to the work of power-hungry humans in pursuit of war. The wolf had firsthand knowledge of the many faces of evil. For he had seen it all. Now he was alerted to an Evil growing larger around him. Would he be in need of the angels? His instinct would tell him soon enough when he appeared.

# Chapter 35

It was late in the evening when Harry showed up at Maureen's apartment building. Joe was at his usual perch when Harry acknowledged him and asked that he call Maureen. He had not called her earlier when he found himself unmindful of the fact he was driving to her apartment. Harry inquired if everything seemed to be alright with her. Joe had just observed she hadn't been her usual self the past few days, and she asked that I take Max out the past couple of days, which is not like her.

"She asked that you come on up, Harry."

"Thanks, Joe."

Harry was greeted with a smile and hug saved only for him.

"I'm so glad to see you," greeted Maureen.

A shadow was lifted from her demeanor. She was not alone.

"Have you eaten?" she asked.

"Yes, I'm fine. Look, I want to talk to you about something." Harry as usual was trusting his instinct. "I think it's time we told your uncle your concerns, and that you're the reason I contacted him."

Her face drained. "Oh Harry how can I tell him it's my sister, his niece, is the reason I fear for his life. There, I actually said it out loud. What if I'm wrong?"

"Yes, but what if you're right. I've met your sister. She sends chills down my spine. I think she would be capable of anything. You said it yourself, you know what she's thinking and feeling. John needs to know, and if she is planning something it's better that he does know. He must not be caught off guard. There is no one out there that has a grudge or vendetta against him. He's a good man and deserves to know, especially if it may be a member of his family. And you can't go on like this."

"There's also another component to this," he continued. "Nora is wearing an emerald bracelet that is a one-of-a-kind piece of jewelry. It was stolen from a woman who was assaulted and put in the hospital. I noticed it on her arm. I had to make sure. That's when I took her out. The woman attacked was a patient of the surgeon your sister worked for. That robbery was worth millions. Josh gave me the insurance file last week. There is a connection."

Harry asked, "Is your sister capable of something like this?"

Maureen looked at him beaten. She sighed heavily, knowing this was something she did not want to admit to herself. For so many years, she had uncanny feelings about the bad things that happened in her life, especially the death of her parents. Deep down she always blamed Nora.

It was late in the evening when Harry showed up at Maureen's apartment building. Joe was at his usual perch when Harry acknowledged him and asked that he call Maureen. He had not called her earlier when he found himself unmindful of the fact he was driving to her apartment. Harry inquired if everything seemed to be alright with her. Joe had just observed she hadn't been her usual self the past few days, and she asked that I take Max out the past couple of days, which is not like her.

"She asked that you come on up, Harry."

"Thanks, Joe."

Harry was greeted with a smile and hug saved only for him.

"I'm so glad to see you," greeted Maureen.

A shadow was lifted from her demeanor. She was not alone.

"Have you eaten?" she asked.

"Yes, I'm fine. Look, I want to talk to you about something." Harry as usual was trusting his instinct. "I think it's time we told your uncle your concerns, and that you're the reason I contacted him."

Her face drained. "Oh Harry how can I tell him it's my sister, his niece, is the reason I fear for his life. There, I actually said it out loud. What if I'm wrong?"

"Yes, but what if you're right. I've met your sister. She sends chills down my spine. I think she would be capable of anything. You said it yourself, you know what she's thinking and feeling. John needs to know, and if she is planning something it's better that he does know. He must not be caught off guard. There is no one out there that has a grudge or vendetta against him. He's a good man and deserves to know, especially if it may be a member of his family. And you can't go on like this."

"There's also another component to this," he continued. "Nora is wearing an emerald bracelet that is a one-of-a-kind piece of jewelry. It was stolen from a woman who was assaulted and put in the hospital. I noticed it on her arm. I had to make sure. That's when I took her out. The woman attacked was a patient of the surgeon your sister worked for. That robbery was worth millions. Josh gave me the insurance file last week. There is a connection."

Harry asked, "Is your sister capable of something like this?"

Maureen looked at him beaten. She sighed heavily, knowing this was something she did not want to admit to herself. For so many years, she had uncanny feelings about the bad things that happened in her life, especially the death of her parents. Deep down she always blamed Nora.

# Chapter 36

She had been unable to sleep at all the last three nights. Cold chills and a dark foreboding haunted her throughout the night. It doggedly held on through her workday. Even the job that she loved so much could not release her from the terror that clutched at her throat. She needed sleep.

Harry retrieved a bottle of brandy from the shelf and poured her a good two ounces, and one for himself. This time he did not let her fall asleep on the sofa. He scooped her up in his arms and took her to her bed. She lay quietly in his embrace. The brandy and his nearness calmed her. Her body lay warmly beside him, and she slept. He stroked her hair, and he was awash with emotion. Harry was slowly developing a deep hate for whoever or whatever was doing this to her. When he was sure she was asleep, he covered her gently and kissed her.

Without disturbing her he watched the soft breathing in and out of her breast and retreated to a comfortable chair in the other room after pouring himself another good shot of brandy. Now he couldn't sleep. Max kept him company. In the wee hours of the morning, she cried out. Harry rushed to the bedroom facing a panic-stricken woman, eyes wide open with fright. The terror had left her face drained of all color and breathing heavily.

Frantically she reached out for the solace of his arms. He held on tight whispering words of comfort. He would have held her like that forever. Finally, he felt the rigidness of her body relax, and her breathing returned to normal, she broke from his embrace and stared at him.

"Harry, I saw her, I saw Nora, only it wasn't Nora. Something horrible is going to happen, and I don't know when and I don't know how." Her fear turned to anger and then fear again

"My family is in danger, and I'm helpless."

"We're going to figure this out, Maureen. First things first. You're going to call your uncle tomorrow and tell him everything you know and feel. You are not betraying your sister or your family, and he deserves to know."

"You're right Harry, I can't live like this. These visions are getting worse, I can't work, and I can't sleep."

She again nestled into the protectiveness of his arms. Desire swept over them, but tonight they did not have the luxury of passion. Their love could wait.

# Chapter 37

"Uncle John. I need to talk to you." She caught him early at his plant.

"It's important. Can you meet me for lunch today?"

"Certainly honey, you sound distressed. Is everything Ok with you?"

"Yes, I'm fine, but this is important, and I must ask you not to say anything to anyone about meeting me."

"How about the club at noon?"

"No, Uncle John, how about that little restaurant you and Diane took me to? The club is nice, but Conrad and Nora still frequent it quite a lot, don't they? And it is a bit of a rumor mill of who's who and where and how who met who. I would feel far better if we met at Diane's choice."

"Alright Honey whatever you say, not a word to anyone."

"I'll see you at noon."

John was puzzled. It was unusual for Maureen to call like that. They had lunch before, but not under such cloak and dagger theater. John was sincerely hoping everything was good with her. He was actually looking forward to the little restaurant he and Diane would frequent. It was her favorite. A feeling of nostalgia and loss captured him for the moment, and then a half-smile of all the good times he and Diane shared there together.

At 11:30, John pulled out of his lot only to meet Nora pulling in. Agitated, he reluctantly stopped as she pulled up beside his window.

"Hi Uncle John, I thought I would drop in and say hello to see if you needed any help and catch up on your new projects."

"Well, I can't today, I have an appointment."

"Oh, well I'll just go in and say hello to everyone for a minute.  I'll see you tonight."

John nodded his head and hurried off, scolding himself for being rude to her. He also noted his recent behavior was very unlike him.

When John left the office, Laurie, his reception-ist, and assistant was still at her desk. He was never the secretive sort and had always left his office door open, but for some reason, today he felt compelled to lock it.

He was glad he did, when suddenly, coming from some unknown voice in his head, he checked behind him to see he wasn't followed. Silly, too much caffeine. John dismissed such paranoia. He had been edgy and not himself this past week. He again thought of Maureen, hoping everything was fine with her.

# Chapter 38

When John entered the restaurant a wave of nostalgia overtook him bringing a smile to his face. He remembered why Diane liked it so much. It was bright and cheery with an atrium cascading with greenery. He spied Maureen's table and walked toward her with a broad smile. He was pleasantly surprised by Harry. Harry stood to shake his hand.

"Surprised to see me?"

"Well yes, and a little confused."

The waitress appeared. Harry suggested, "John, better order up a double scotch. I'll have the same for me." When the waitress retreated Harry wasted no time addressing John's obvious bafflement.

"About three weeks ago I received a call from Josh Lawton, your attorney. He was approached by someone who had a unique problem, under difficult circumstances. She had no place to go, knowing the authorities wouldn't help her and all the doctors, and shrinks in the world would not take her seriously. Josh and I have dealt with shall we say less than normal cases before. I am his private investigator also dealing with insurance fraud."

"Go on" John was completely immersed.

"Josh sent her to me."

"Oh, Uncle John, it was me," Maureen broke in. "I'm scared to death your life is in danger."

Maureen took the floor. "I am not crazy or mentally unbalanced, I knew you wouldn't take me seriously, but I wanted you to be on guard for anything. I am going half-crazy thinking, no feeling, I mean feeling you're in terrible danger. I can't sleep. I can't work. I have visions, nightmares. They have been increasing, becoming more vivid. It's Nora Uncle John, it's Nora. Harry said it's time I tell you. I have no proof but I know it's her."

John sat there, silent. He saw the pain in his niece's eyes, with an understanding of how difficult this must have been to tell him this.

"Maureen, you are distraught, what put these foolish thoughts in your head?"

He looked up and motioned for the waitress again and indicated another of the same. Harry nodded also, pointing to his glass for a refill. Maureen nursed her glass of wine.

"Nora?" He refrained from saying "I can't believe this. Nora would hurt me? My niece?"

"No, Uncle John, look at me. Look at me. No, Uncle John, I mean Nora will KILL you.

"This is nonsense!"

Confusion and disbelief engulfed his face, then turned to concern for Maureen.

"Honey," he reached out for her hand. "Whatever possessed you to have these awful thoughts about your sister?" She looked helplessly at Harry.

"John, I believe her, I don't know why, or how it can be proven but John, something else, I don't know how this is connected. Nora has a bracelet that was recently stolen from an emerald collection. The night I took her out, she wore it. It was one of a kind. It was stolen from a patient who was assaulted and landed in the hospital. The collection is worth millions. She worked for the surgeon who was this woman's plastic surgeon. John, is she capable of attacking someone? Is this just a coincidence?"

"Hmm, Nora did say that she lost her job. She didn't quite seem herself, and she did mention she had not heard from her boyfriend, that fellow Johnny Polo, for a while. He was out of town on business. She actually gave me the idea there might be a wedding in sight. She seemed quite happy."

He turned his attention back on Maureen and his concern for her. Imploring her to remove these foolish thoughts about her sister and make sense.

Harry again motioned for the waitress for another round, who by this time had given up on trying to get an order for lunch.

Maureen, after living in this hell for so many years, decided it was time to let it all out. "Uncle John, I beg you to listen to me and do not be dismissive of me. For years I have carried shame and guilt with me, and even fear." John was listening now with full attention. "Nora is my sister, my twin, she emphasized. There are times, I feel what she feels, know what she's thinking, know if she's injured. As children, I always knew where she was hiding. She was a bully, she would steal, manipulate and cheat. I grew up with her, we lived together, believe me, I know. I was the victim of her deceit. It was useless. Our parents would not believe me if I accused her.

Uncle John," she looked at him imploringly, "when we lost our parents, and you took the three of us in, I could not get over the feeling she had something to do with it. It haunts me to this day.  When she married and moved away twice, the distance seemed to give me relief. When she came back, her living here was disruptive and unsettling to me."

She continued, "And when Diane died, I couldn't bear to stay there. There was no reason for Diane's death. Uncle John, didn't you find her death at the very least under strange circumstances?"

John just sat there, stoic, in deep thought.

"There have been times, I worried about my own safety," she confided.

John stirred, trying to digest what Maureen had just told him.

Maureen began again. "I love you, Uncle John, I know this is hard to hear, but I do not want anything to happen to you."

John looked at her lovingly and took her hand in his.

"She's dangerous now, I can feel her strength. She lost her two meal tickets from the marriage. You have curtailed her credit card use. Now you tell me she's lost her job. Harry said she told him her fiancé gave her the bracelet. Now you say she has not heard from him.

That may explain this unbelievable anger and hate I feel from her. I dream of infernos' and death, destruction and your face is in every one of them, Uncle John.

"This is not good," she added.

The waitress made another attempt at their order. They all were spent and drained from too much alcohol and conversation. It was time they all got something in their stomach. Overcoming John's skepticism and reluctance to believe was the hardest part of this meeting. His recent paranoia and Nora's smothering interest in the plant and its projects, plus her nagging interest in helping with the company books fueled his desire to accept Maureen's accusation. John also mentioned that Nora wanted to talk about the family business and its plan for the future. Over dinner, Harry saw an opening. They needed a plan to draw Nora out.

It was after 5:00 when they left the restaurant. Harry made sure John was able to drive, he and Maureen left leaving John with another reminder to stay alert. Harry would call him tomorrow. John took a long ride to gain perspective on all that had been discussed before he pulled in his driveway. He was hoping he could avoid Nora tonight.

He went directly to his study and locked the door.

# Chapter 39

This preposterous seed of Maureen's accusation started to take root. He poured himself another drink and sat in his comfortable chair. He was tired, but he knew there would be no sleeping tonight. He reached for the remote to catch up on the news when the sound of distant wind chimes echoed in his ear. It drew him to the doors leading to Diane's greenhouse and garden. Twilight was dying, and soft shadows danced throughout the great glass greenhouse.

Walking down the garden path, John was at peace with his memories as he was enticed by the haunting sound of the chimes. He sat down by Diane's fountain of cherubs reveling in his memories of her, when softly from the shadows The Wolf appeared before him. He was frozen in fear when the animal moved silently towards him and gazed into his eyes.

The fear quickly subsided and an incredible feeling of well-being washed over him. John was secure that the animal would not harm him. The deep blue eyes of the old wolf continued his gaze into the heart and soul of John, who found himself in a total state of content and awareness. As if urging him to stay, the wolf extended his paw and turned into the shadows only to return and lay two large dead copperheads at his feet.

# Chapter 40

Returning to his study after his lengthy, clandestine meeting with a wolf, he was met with the pounding at his door of Nora. Uncle John, Uncle John, are you in there.

He answered, "Yes, give me a moment."

He opened the study door but cut her shy of entering.

"Are you ok uncle? I was beginning to get worried."

"I'm fine Nora, I just came in from the garden from a stroll."

She strained her neck to see inside his sanctuary.

"If I can help you with anything, Uncle, just let me know. I have more time now since my temp job has ended."

Completely composed, John thanked her for her concern and said he was going to turn in shortly. "I've been thinking about the business and my health, and where we may be headed in the future. It may involve quite a bit of updating and retooling. That means a substantial investment on my part. Just trying to work a few things out. Why don't we have dinner tomorrow night and talk about it?"

"That would be great Uncle John." She reached up to hug him good night and told him how much she looked forward to collaborating with him. It was then he saw the bracelet and commented on what a beautiful piece it was.

"Diane always loved unique pieces," he commented to Nora. "Get that from the fella you're going to marry?" He added casually. "You'll have to bring him over so we can meet him." All just casual chit-chat on John's part. "Now go on, I'll be along. Going to watch the news, and we'll talk tomorrow."

Smiling, she sweetly told her uncle how much she loved him and how much she looked forward to collaborating with him about their business and said goodnight.

Alone and unmasked, a scowl stole over her face with deep hate for everyone around her. She had been unable to contact Johnny Polo, it had been days, calls went straight to voicemail. May he rot in hell, and everyone else with him.

# Chapter 41

They met at 9 o'clock in Josh Lawton's office. Three coffees black sat steaming before them. Harry had spoken to Josh earlier and brought him up to speed about this lunch with Maureen and John's obvious reluctance to accept such nonsense as he called it.

When John entered the room, Harry saw a different man. He was confident, full of purpose, and when he addressed the other two men, there were absolutely no reservations about Maureen's revelation yesterday about Nora. He was no longer a fragile and grieving man.

John turned to Harry and thanked him heartily for trying to protect him, realizing how difficult it had to be, to believe such an outlandish story that Maureen brought to him.

"She just wanted you to be safe sir."

"Oh, and by the way, I love your niece," Harry said.

A broad grin stole over John's face, the same for Josh, who could not be more surprised, thinking he would always be the one that got away.

"Alright, just felt I had to get that out of the way. Now, where were we?"

John went on, "Harry, you and I talked about drawing Nora out. I've told her I'm making some changes to the business, updating, and retooling the plant. I said we would discuss it over dinner tonight. What I didn't tell her is that I would like you and Josh as my attorney and Maureen and Carlton to be there. Josh, I know my will with Diane gone needs to be updated."

"That's true John."

"I'm counting on you all coming to dinner tonight. I'll have Cook make something special. I think Nora is not going to be happy with my plans for the business and choice for trustee. Oh, and tell me more about this bracelet. I did see it."

Josh had the file conveniently in his desk drawer. He pulled it out, and John paged through the inventory.

"There, that looks like it," pointing it out as John spoke.

Harry chimed in "that's secondary right now, John. First, we are concerned about your safety."

"I know you are Harry. When you see Maureen, tell her I'm sorry I didn't believe her."

"John, I didn't believe it at first. I still am not sure about this whole thing. We're basing all this worry and talk on bad dreams!"

"What makes you so sure now, John? What has turned you around?"

John looked him squarely in the eye. "You wouldn't believe me if I told you."

"Try me."

"Got another cup of that coffee?" Josh's assistant appeared with more coffee. All three cups were filled.

"Alright now John, what's made you so sure about this?"

John again looked him directly in the eye with resolve. There was an uncomfortable pause before John lowered his head in submission to what he was about say. "You heard me right. A wolf," he cried in a voice an octave higher.

"Last night, I was scared to death. After leaving you and Maureen yesterday, I went into my study, and as you might think, I was in a state of shock and confusion, not understanding any of this," John began. "I was sitting there quietly when I was drawn to my wife's garden. It was as if I was being called by the sound of music or the wind ringing bells."

John went on, the other two men as silent as the night. "The greenhouse was filled with silence and shadows, and I was alone with the memories of Diane. It was a perfect evening. I sat by the fountain she had installed last year, recalling how she loved spending time out here with her flowers and plants, and Max. He was always by her side. Then gentlemen," he interrupted himself. "Remove yourself from our reality for the moment. I became aware of the soft padding of feet beside me. Looking around, it was the sight of a wolf that rendered me paralyzed. It came toward me with its head lowered, then looked into my eyes and put my fears to rest. The animal calmed me."

John continued his story, "I was literally frozen in fear, but it was not there to harm me. I felt it. He was a massive beast, but he had no intent to hurt me, only to relieve me of any pain or doubts.

After regaining my composure, I had this incredible feeling of peace fall over me. This animal actually talked to me, well, not talk, but communicated with me. It was as if he asked me to stay, he had things I needed to know. He was here to help me. This Wolf extended his paw, left for just moments, and returned with two dead snakes. They were huge copperheads, the snake venom that killed my Diane, and laid them at my feet," John said still incredulously.

Wrapping up his story, John told them, "I sat by that animal for what seemed to be hours before I went back inside. I could not have felt more clear-eyed or enlightened in my entire life. You are now looking at a man who believes in fairy tales and unicorns."

There was silence for a few short moments among the three men digesting this fantastic story. It was Josh who broke the silence, looking directly at Harry. Then he looked at John. "I believe you, John, we both do."

"You do?"

"Let's just say my wife's sister and her husband had a similar experience, and it involved a wolf. Something we don't always talk about, because it is so fantastic, and unbelievable, but I believe you. Someday I'll tell you about it. Now, what time do you want us for dinner?"

They quickly renewed their conversation about John's plans for the dinner tonight and the parts they all play.

# Chapter 42

Johnny Polo was having the time of his life. But still aware that the high profile and value of these jewels brought with them many problems. He knew he could not get too comfortable. So far, he was scot-free. Dumb Nora had no idea that he was involved. He had no reason to believe there were any suspects, and he was relieved that the Breckenridge dame had recovered. Johnny Polo was set for the rest of his life if he played his cards right.

He had plenty of cash in the safe, and yet he still burned it up enjoying the high life. Johnny was a small fish in this game, and he knew it. He did not like to take chances. These jewels were all too fresh to try and fence through the small-time players he knew. Time was his friend and patience was his enemy. If he could keep his cool, and be discreet he may hear of some names able to handle such a prize, but he was not going to do it lying on the beach. How ironic, Johnny had to go back to work.

Maybe he should go legit and set up shop somewhere on an island, sit on the jewels for years, and sell the stones one by one. Ahh, but Johnny knew, he was much too young and flamboyant for that. He wanted to see the world. The tools of his trade, charm, and wit lay fallow for too long. He needed information and inroads to the right people and the right circles. Ok, Johnny, the ladies are waiting. Inwardly he smiled to himself.

This great wealth was becoming a burden.

# Chapter 43

Conrad certainly didn't expect a call from his uncle for dinner. They had barely spoken since he was fired from the plant, and there were no family dinners at home, at least since Diane died. The old man even seemed pleasant on the phone, said he had something of importance to talk to him about and would like him to show by six. Curiosity more than anything would bring him to the table. He was at his uncle's club when John called and told him he would be there in about an hour. Maureen and Harry met at Josh's office and they all left from there.

Nora had been out shopping, looking forward to meeting with her Uncle tonight. This was the time tonight to cement her plans for her eventual control of the business. John had clearly lost interest in the plant and was unable to continue with Diane gone.

She had been one big impediment and problem for her. Getting Diane out of the way for the inheritance and allowed her uncle to rely on her for support and comfort. This was essential that she gain his trust.

Breezing through the door, caught up in her web of controlling thoughts, she was caught up short by the sight of her siblings and Harry sitting comfortably in the living room having a drink. The face of Josh was familiar, but she could not recall who he was.

"Well, we're all here now", John announced, "We can eat."

Nora had not recovered from this unexpected turn of events. She excused herself for the moment to put away the packages, while John herded everyone into the dining room. Nora quickly retreated to her bedroom to deal with her out-of-control emotion. She struggled to keep her demons at bay. It was like a monster facing the rays of the first light of daybreak or a full moon. Nora must not let them see her like this. Not now, but soon, they would all be out of the picture. Uncle, sister, she may need her brother, for now. These thoughts brought joy to her, stunting the transformation she was experiencing.

Her countenance returned with a sweetness to smile, erasing every wrinkle and imperfection. Relaxed, she powdered her nose and returned to the guests.

# Chapter 44

As promised, dinner was exceptional. All experienced good wine and food, coupled with quiet and interesting conversation. Nora, of course, knew everyone but had to be reintroduced to Josh. It had been many years and then she had only met him once. She also made it a point to sit by Harry, across from her sister, throughout dinner. John had made it a point, not to disrupt his plans.

When dessert was finished, and the wine was poured, John prepared to let his family know what changes may be ahead. He directed his thoughts to Nora, Maureen, and Conrad.

"I have already spoken to Josh about my wishes. Since Diane is no longer here, it was necessary to make some changes. The business will be expanding.. We have had several new contracts, one a small government one, but the plant will need some updating and retooling. This will require a substantial investment on my part. Special insurance, required by the government, and coverage of new equipment and any upgrading and changes to the plant. We are working on a new prototype for a small part of the landing gear."

John looked at Conrad and said, "I know you have shown no desire or real interest in the business. However, as my nephew, you will receive the benefits of its profits, and, of course, the home. Josh will handle all inventory of the plant, the home, and the property. It will be covered in the trust.

Speaking to the group, John continued, "It is unfortunate that Tom could not make it this evening. I think you all know him. He has been with me for almost thirty years. He will continue to head the plant, in the event of my death. Nora, you will benefit as Conrad. Maureen, obviously you have never married, and certainly have proven yourself as having good business sense. You will be the executor of the trust, and Tom will report to you quarterly."

"And, oh yes, since you are the eldest," he chuckled, "even if it is by several hours, it falls to you. There is a lot of work to be done, and it is going to take some time to get resolved, but I wanted to be assured that you all knew what plans were for everyone's future. I'm just sorry Diane is not here to share. We had many plans to travel and enjoy.

There was a short period of silence around the table while everything was thoughtfully measured. Maureen, of course, looked to her uncle for reassurance that he had made the right decision.

When the decision has finally been made, John assured Maureen," I always trust myself to have made the right decision. You'll do fine honey. But I don't plan to go anywhere too soon."

He smiled at her and hugged her, telling her at the same time he loved her and was sorry that he ever doubted her. "I know you had my best interest at heart."

Conrad came up to his uncle, shook his hand, said thank you, and got out of there as soon as possible. He had a date. A wealthy woman in the city who liked the athletic type.

Nora looked at this nauseating scene unfolding before her and cursed the wretched woman that was her sister but went to her, to show her support. At least she knew what she must do later.

Nora quickly turned her attention to Harry who was begging Josh to get us out of here as soon as you can.

"Harry, it's so nice to see you again," cooed Nora, "Have you been too busy to call me?"

Taking him firmly by the arm she pulled herself to him. "I would love to see you again,"

Harry could play this game too, as he whispered to her, "I would love to see you again too, but the next few days are going to be difficult. I have several business situations that need my attention. Why don't I call you next week, and we will get together. Tonight, Josh and I have a few things to go over. Your sister met him at his office, and they are my ride back."

As Josh looked his way, he took that as his cue to extract himself from Nora. Taking her by the hand Harry promised to call. With that, Harry quickly left, joining Maureen and Josh. He thanked John for the dinner on their way out.

Without giving Nora a chance to engage him in a question-and-answer period, John said goodnight to her and excused himself to his study to finish up some paperwork. Nora was left in a bewildered and dark mood that was quickly turning lethal. Nora's fortunes were changing, and she was not going to allow that to happen.

John sat back in his chair, a changed man. He had been walking around this past year in a daze. Diane would not have wanted that. She would not have allowed it.

He was a man reborn, a man with a purpose. Now that he had poked the hornet's nest, he must stay alert and sleep with one eye open.

The Wolf stood watch, alone and silent sentry.

# Chapter 45

osh dropped Harry and Maureen off and said goodnight. The night was still young when they walked into the vestibule of her apartment and greeted Joe.

Harry sent Maureen ahead to the elevator, while he took Joe aside telling him he was planning to spend the night, she had a few rough nights this past week.  Joe seemed to understand. He had taken a shine to Harry, so he nodded as if giving his approval.

"You take care of her Mr. Quinn he whispered, and anything I can do let me know."

"I'll do my best Joe."

"Oh. And I just took Max out a while ago." "

"Thanks, Joe."  He caught up with her at the elevator indicating he had Joe's blessing to watch over Maureen.

"I'm happy you're staying. I don't think my uncle's announcement tonight met with my sister's approval. My senses of premonition were on overdrive. We might have all put ourselves in jeopardy."

"I'm inclined to agree with you," Harry answered.

They took the elevator to her floor hand in hand. His presence gave her comfort. The burden she carried alone, unable to share with anyone over the years was lifted.

She confided in him fully now. "I know something terrible is going to happen, Harry, I just don't know when or how. I know I'm repeating myself, but Uncle John really doesn't know what she is capable of."

"Maureen, he is completely on board with this. He now believes you about everything. Can't you tell he's a changed man? He talked to Josh and me. He won't turn his back on her." Harry spoke in a soothing voice, "Now I want you to try and relax. I'll pour you some wine, and I'll make that buttered popcorn that you like so well. We'll watch a movie. "Ok?"

"Ok," Maureen replied.

When Harry closed the door behind them, he had made up his mind, there was no staring longingly into each other's eyes, or casual flirtations. There was no planning, just doing. He simply took her in his arms and kissed her. Like a man who had never known love. And it was true. For the first and last time, Harry Quinn was in love.

He met with no resistance, and he knew she felt the same. Slowly he caressed and held her, feeling for the first time, the meaning and power of real love. Quietly without a word, he lifted her high, then falling into his arms he carried her to bed. Silently, passion stole the hours. Gentleness and patience were swept away by fulfillment of raw desire. There was no tonight and no tomorrow. Only now.

There would be no popcorn tonight.

# Chapter 46

The demons inside her would not be quelled. Nora could not enter the garden from her uncle's study. So, entering from the far side of the greenhouse beyond the gate, she called out to her minion consulates, and when she found there was no answer to her call, she followed the path beneath the great greenhouse only to find her pets lying in an entangled and silent bloody mass. They were no more. Seeing them lying dead beneath her feet, a blackness overtook her and she vowed all the fires of hell to consume those who did this. They all would pay. She contrived a curse on her family and all surrounding them. In the name of Satan and all that's evil, pain and suffering would bear fruit within their lives and spread. No longer hidden, the wrath of the demon was fully exposed.

Nora's greed was in full flower, she began planning a curious death for her Uncle John's demise. Storming from the greenhouse, a full night had fallen. The moon was high and bright. Shadows lurked at every burrow and branch of the landscape. It was then that her blood ran cold. The sound of a low and menacing growl stole over her, eclipsing all her thoughts of chaos, death, and destruction. Fear was now her driving force.

She whirled around only to see a large silken head with great piercing eyes penetrating her soul. Alone, she realized, it was just her and the wolf. Reflections of the moon beamed carelessly off the animal's fangs, and the great beast remained rooted to the hillside, staring at her, daring her to move. She stood there powerless, when the night wind quickly gained strength, brewing itself into a lonesome howl. And then, just as quickly as the beast appeared, he was gone.

Shaken, Nora had just experienced a power and force she had never encountered. She did not take it lightly. She recovered quickly from the incident and returned to the main house. Ignoring the closed door of the study, she retired to her room, and for the remainder of the night, she began plotting a course for destruction. His death must be seen as an accident.

And all the while, the haunting specter of the Wolf dogged her.

Maureen slept soundly while Harry and Max completed the dog's morning routine. When they returned, Harry was laden with hot coffee and goodies. He even had a cup for Joe when he returned, who was perched at his station as usual.

Joe greeted Harry warmly and thankfully accepted his coffee.

"You know Mr. Quinn, it's the little things in life that make us happy" as he raised his cup in a mock salute. "Have a good day Joe."

In the apartment, dog and man found Maureen still resting comfortably, but stirring slightly.

"You," she murmured, "let me sleep too long." She reached greedily for the coffee he brought. "Ohhhh, that's so good." The hot liquid was bringing her to life.

"I have got to get to work," She announced.

"Not so fast. Are you sure you're up to it?"

"Harry, I have been consumed by this whole situation. Couldn't work. Couldn't sleep. But I love my job, and I've been neglecting it. I feel so much better now that it's out in the open, and Uncle John is convinced, and frankly, now that you're here. I know there's still a part of you that thinks this is foolishness."

"Well, that's true, but I've come a long way from where I was."

"And Uncle John? How did you convince him?"

"Let's just say he had a little help. I'll tell you all about it sometime. Now, if you're going to work I am making a date with your sister. She thinks I'm adorable, can't get enough of me he quipped. Hopefully, I can get an idea of what's going on in that head of hers, and anything about her boyfriend and the bracelet. Did she talk to you at all about him?"

"I haven't really talked to her too much since I moved out. She did call a couple of times, just to talk. She said she met him at a bar. It's a new place, I forget the name, but she did go on and on about him when we spoke. His name was Johnny and his last name was Polo. I remember because it was so unusual. She did tell me he was a little younger than her, but that didn't seem to bother him at all."

"When did she get the temp job at the doctor's office?"

"Not sure, but after her last divorce. When she came home, she was broke and depressed, and of course, Uncle John and Diane welcomed her. They helped 'til she got back on her feet. Uncle John gave her a little to do at the plant like he did Conrad. Diane tried to get her involved with her clubs and social work. I loved Diane, but she and Nora just didn't click.

Maureen continued, "After Diane died, I just couldn't bear to be around there. Uncle John was crushed. He just couldn't navigate without Diane. I was working, and Nora just settled back in, like when we were kids. Since she came back, old feelings and suspicions started in on me, not too bad at first, but eventually drove me to Josh and subsequently you. Harry be careful. She's older now, stronger, and more capable. You cannot trust her. Take it from me who has lived with her through the early years, and high school. No one believed me then and no one believes me now."

She put her arms around him and pulled him close. "I couldn't stand it if anything happened to you."

"If I could throw a bucket of water on her and she would melt, I would."

"She's still my sister.  I wish she would get married again and move to Alaska. Now go on."

She pushed him away. "Don't get me all sentimental and gooey again. I've got to call the office and get to work. You go see what you can do about her."

Harry hugged her tightly and said he would be back tonight.

"I look forward to it. I love having you here with me. Oh, and a nice bottle of wine and Chinese would be nice. I haven't gone to the store in days."

Harry grinned at her, patted Max on the head, and left the apartment the happiest he has been in a long, long time.

He loved being domesticated.

# Chapter 47

Harry walked into his office and kissed Tiffany, his loyal girl Friday on the forehead. She had been mother hen, mother confessor, confident and all-around great assistant over the years. Waltzing in the door, he smugly announced to her that she had finally gotten her wish.

"Don't tell me, let me guess, You're in love!"

"Does it show?"

"Well I'm happy for you, boss, it's about time! It has to be Ms. Bradford."

"How'd you know?"

"Oh, come on boss. You always acted un-Harry-like around her. Your jaw dropped. And you couldn't speak."

"That noticeable?"

"Um-Hm, she responded, shaking her head. Again, I'm happy for you."

"You're a jewel, Tiffany."

He fell back into his hard-boiled private eye investigator mode, asking her for the insurance file on the jewel collection Satan's fire.  He retired to his office while she retrieved it.

"Thanks, Tiff."

While thumbing through the less than complete file, he phoned Nora, asking what her plans were for tomorrow night. He had no intention of leaving Maureen tonight. Nora could wait.

She answered her cell, obviously surprised to hear from him, but still eager to accept his invitation to dinner. Their conversation was not long, almost business-like, but Nora had plans for Harry Quinn that definitely were anything but business-like. Unwittingly, Harry had also taken her mind off deadly plans plotted for her sister and Uncle for the moment. There was so much hate and resentment growing in Nora, that she barely thought of anything but revenge for Johnny Polo and her family. Where to begin first. She had no doubt their time would come, but for now, her attentions were all directed to Harry. Insurance and securities, that was his game. She needed to know more.

For now. though, a day at the spa was needed. Surely her credit card would allow that. And Harry, for the most part, spent his day updating the Satan's Fire file. The police had yet to have a solid lead. And Josh knew nothing more from the insurance firm and their bird dogs. Tiffany came up with nothing from any of Harry's "men on the street" Pawn shops, dealers, high-end fences.  So far, as they say, it had been a clean getaway, which reminded him, he had to figure out a way to extricate himself from Nora tomorrow night.

He left the office around five with a big fat zero regarding the emeralds. The only link to the heist was one lovely and lonely bracelet encircling a "witch's" arm, but he would deal with that tomorrow. In the meantime, He picked up a bottle of Merlot, a plum dessert wine, and an assortment of Chinese dishes, dumplings, egg rolls, etc. He didn't know her favorite yet, but he was going to enjoy finding out. She was there waiting for him. Harry greeted her, grinning from ear to ear.

Where had that hard-boiled Harry disappeared to?  Ain't love grand!

# Chapter 48

When Harry left Maureen this morning, she was fully up to speed about his plans for this evening, and he would be calling John when he got to the office about his date with Nora.

Harry had prepared Nora for another early evening, as he had out-of-town clients coming in, and had several loose ends he had to take care of, again. Nora seemed a little disappointed. She still had not heard from Johnny but at this point, she would take what she could get. She would deal with Johnny, one way or the other. Besides, she had called Conrad and wanted to meet him somewhere away from the house. Tomorrow will be good. There was much to be done before all this will and trust nonsense was complete. She had not seen much of her Uncle since their so-called family dinner. He always left early for the plant, and did not return until late, and then went straight to his study. Tonight, he returned about 7:00, just about the time Harry was picking her up. In fact, she kissed him lovingly on his cheek as she was going out the door with Harry.

"Good night Uncle John, I'll be home early,"

John could no longer bear the sight of his niece. He knew now that she was responsible for Diane's death, and his brother's. It was not only Maureen's fear for his safety and revelation to him about her sister's deadly deceit and what she was capable of but the altogether unbelievable appearance of a wolf. The protective custody of this wolf was no fairy tale. The animal was here to right an incredible wrong. John marveled at how Good and Evil can come calling, masquerading in so many unthinkable guises. He was hoping Good would come calling tonight. He might be hungry.

Harry took her to a quaint little restaurant, in the local community, not too far from home. Nora was dressed to kill, however, was perfectly satisfied with her escort and his choice for the evening.

"I hope you enjoy this," Harry said to her. "It has a great reputation for steak and seafood.

They sat, and he ordered an excellent bottle of wine, and after small talk, Harry took the lead.

"Nora, you'll have to excuse my reluctance to call. It was all that talk about your fiancée, you know, Johnny was it?"

"I haven't heard from him in well over a week since I dropped him at the airport."

"You haven't? You must be worried sick."

Nora didn't see this uncalled interest in Johnny coming.

"Are you sure he's OK?"

If only to convince Harry, Nora displayed mock concern. "Yes, yes I am. I haven't been able to contact him."

"You've left messages? I left several messages, the beginning of last week, then it went to voice-mail, now I get nothing."

"Has this happened before Nora?"

"Well, Johnny does have a habit of misplacing his phone, a lot."

"Did you two have words?"

"Well, things had gotten a little tense between us."

It was apparent Nora was noticeably getting upset by his questioning. Quickly, Harry excused himself for his interest.

"I'm sorry, it's just that I get a little nervous dealing with married women and ladies with fiancés. I didn't mean to pry, but that's what I do. I set up corporate insurance, and investigate insurance loss and fraud.

"What business is he in?"

Nora really wasn't sure. "I really couldn't tell you exactly what Johnny does, but he always speaks of real estate and investment overseas.

Nora was finding the conversation about Johnny interfering with the budding new relationship with Harry.

"Would he have any problems with his business associates?

"Not that I know of."

"When did you say you dropped him at the airport? I'll see if I can help. I have a relationship with the local police. I'll contact the local hospitals and any reports of missing persons. Have you got a picture of this Johnny?"

This evening was turning out to be anything but what Nora expected. Johnny did not like his picture taken, but Nora did manage to get 2 or 3 pictures which she kept in her wallet. She gave one to Harry.

"I'll see what I can find out if only to save my own skin from a jealous fiancée. You know Nora, a man does not give a bracelet like the one you showed me to just anybody. Those were beautifully matched emeralds. That was not a token gift. I've recovered and seen too many insurance claims for quality gems. He must love you very much, and I do not want to face the jealousy of an angry husband or fiancée. Been there, done that."

Harry Changed the subject, "Now, what sounds good to you on the menu tonight?"

Well Nora, surprise surprise, surprise. This is a man with integrity and old-world values. She smiled demurely and thanked him for all his help. She ordered the Surf and Turf.

Nora was then chauffeured gallantly and charmingly home without a hint of what just happened.

# Chapter 49

Conrad met Nora for a late breakfast at their uncle's club. She was cheerful and for the most part pleasant. Even so, Conrad was always suspicious of her invitations. There was something premeditated about them. From the time they were kids, she would almost always drag him into her schemes to stir up problems for one of her girlfriends or beat up a boyfriend, cheat on a test or retrieve information.

Unlike Maureen, he had not completely detached himself from his sister's bad influence. He knew she was always good for coming up with extra money when he was running low. Especially now when his athletic future was not looking so rosy. So when they were comfortably seated, and Conrad had several Bloody Mary's, did Nora ask him about his feelings about Uncle John's trust and his choice of   Maureen as administrator and CEO of the company.

"What do you mean, what do I feel? What can you do, it's his choice."

"What do you mean it's his choice?" she lashed back at him. "Maureen has no right. I took care of him, nursed him, and the business, I might add, when Diane died."

Conrad, even in his slightly inebriated state, knew this wasn't true. Nora again was fantasizing about her victimization. John had opened his home to her after she failed her second marriage. John and Diane did everything they could for her including trying to find her a job, which both times she found unappealing. When John turned off the free money, she took that temp job.  At least Conrad had enough moral authority to know he was a leech.

"Oh stop it, Nora, that's not true. Uncle John gave you a little work, let's just say to pay your way. You took advantage of him when he was vulnerable after his loss of Diane." Boy, the alcohol was really talking now. It was unusual for Conrad to usurp Nora's proclamations.

Undaunted by Conrad's dismissal of his and her importance, Nora continued to prime Conrad's sense of entitlement to the family fortune. A silent rage seethed inside her. She knew she must be careful not to overplay her hand. Conrad was weak, he must be convinced he was being treated unfairly.

Before she revealed any more of her plans, she held back, knowing she must move slowly for Conrad to be completely brought on board. He always could be stubborn when it came to crossing his so-called line.

"I've been thinking I should try talking to him about coming back to work at the plant. I haven't been having a lot of luck with my sports resume," Conrad mused.

Retreating into a safer subject for conversation, she asked if he had anyone new in his life, since his last girl. Conrad felt on much safer ground now, simply talking about his social life and any promising nibbles he may have in the future for his athletic abilities. Nora felt the comfort level return to the conversation and she ordered one more round of bloody Marys before they went their separate ways. Nora knew the planning and carrying out of the removal of her uncle and sister would be left up to her. It had been a year since Diane's death, under very unusual circumstances. This family purge cannot bring any suspicion on her.

Conrad had become increasingly reluctant over the years to involve himself in her dramas. She could no longer manipulate him as she once had. Therefore he had become expendable. Fear had worked on him as a child. If necessary, it would work again. She may have a need for him.

Her demons were working overtime tonight, simmering in their devil's brew. They were especially masterful at adding a pinch of caution and patience. She looked forward to working with them again.

# Chapter 50

arry came to his office with a motherlode of information. Before noon he had contacted detective Declue with a picture of Polo, his departure from the airport, his destination, type of business, etc. Also, Josh and anyone else who may have a line on this guy. By the end of the day today or tomorrow, he should know everything there was to know about Johnny Polo if any. The dinner last night garnered far more information than he anticipated, and even his quick exit strategy seemed flawless.

He then called John, first to check on him to see if there were any changes in the family dynamics. Harry was happy with John's response.

"For the first time in well over a year, I've never felt better or more clear-headed. I've avoided Nora for the most part. I really haven't given her a chance for any family communication. I am expecting fire-works soon. When I named Maureen as executor, trustee, and administrator, I felt unadulterated hate in her eyes when she looked at me.

"Make no mistake, Harry, John said, "I've been keeping my eyes wide open, I appreciate your concern."

"Have you made arrangements when you all meet Josh and sign the papers?"

"Tonight, I'll tell Nora and Conrad that we are having another little family dinner on Friday to get everything worked out. Josh said he would be there. You won't have to put yourself through this one, Harry."

"Well thanks, John, escaping the clutches of Nora has become quite challenging. In the mean-time, I've sent out all the information on the brace-let, and the guy that gave it to her. I really don't think Nora has any knowledge that it was stolen. I'll keep you posted, and you be careful. Call me if anything changes. I am now on my way to visit your lovely niece Maureen."

"John had yet to advise Nora and Conrad that the documents had been drawn up and were ready for signature. He had made arrangements to stay in town tonight and would advise them before he left to be here Friday about 6:00. If anyone had any objections or questions regarding his wishes for the business and property settlement, they could voice them then.

Shortly before 8:00 p.m., John knocked on Nora's door asking her to attend another family dinner this Friday, much the same as the one they had before with the addition of his attorney. There were documents to be reviewed and Josh was taking the time to explain to all concerned.

"Please see that your brother is also in attendance. I'll be out of town. But I will be back before dinner." John did not leave much room for chit-chat, he made his announcement and then was gone. Nora was more or less left flat-footed and frantic.

She immediately called Conrad, but there was no answer. They had no more time, those papers could not be finalized. She hurried to John's office and found it locked, although she knew his attorney had all the information. Besides, she just wanted a drink, and she liked his scotch. Reluctantly she poured a straight bourbon and sat down to wait for Conrad.

Patience was a virtue Nora did not possess, the evil within was growing. If Conrad showed any reluctance tonight, he would have a grim reminder of just how powerful big sister could be.

# Chapter 51

Nora wasted no time confronting Conrad as he walked in the door, not completely alert as he could be, and certainly in no mood for Nora's nonsense.

"Where have you been?" she demanded. Her question was met with indifference and silence.

"Time is running out," she screamed. "He's got that attorney coming here again on Friday. He cannot finalize those papers. He has got to be stopped."

Conrad had not made one comment since he walked through the door, not really comprehending what she was hysterically wailing about. He finally reeled around with power and strength in his voice that Conrad seldom displayed. "WE CAN DO NOTHING!" he roared. "Let it be, Nora."

Undaunted by Conrad's suddenly discovered sense of bravado, Nora grew large, her face contorting into a fearful figure, grabbing the now puny Conrad by the throat, reminding him of their blood contract and allegiance.

Tortured memories of the past came vividly back, watching his parents fall beneath a sail and reaching upward for Conrad. He knew he could save them but Nora held fast. She willed the sail to swallow them and would not allow the youth to save them. The memory left him paralyzed with hate and self-loathing as Nora still wielded her power over him.

His thoughts turned to fire and damnation, as his breath was strangled from him and his body left in a breathless heap. The demon's breath blew hot and putrid over him and Its demand was simple, He cannot be allowed to live. The horrendous sight retrieved and left the simpering and breathless Conrad alone with his thoughts. He lay there in a stupor until he regained what sanity he had left. He pulled himself to his feet and poured himself another drink. It had been years since he had experienced her full wrath. Conrad was sure there was more ahead. Over the years, he was able to push the nightmares away. Now, his life had become a nightmare. Nora's transformation was proof. There was no reprieve, help, or escape from tortured sleep. The devil held tight.

He refilled his glass and walked out into the night air. The fresh air and silence calmed him, and viewing the landscape in the soft moonlight, it occurred to him what a really beautiful place this was. He found himself remembering how Diane loved this place and her greenhouse. Uncle John had built her a huge glass-enclosed cathedral, looming over the house with large palm trees and just about every flower and plant known to man. Conrad could almost classify himself as a botanist. Aunt Diane taught him so much about everything that bloomed and grew.

The night enclosed and comforted him, and he found himself drifting with the night wind to the main entrance of the enclosure. He paused as the sweet smell of honeysuckle and the soft sound of wind chimes greeted him from the hillside. In that time to savor the moment, the great beast was beside him. The moon shone silver off his mighty head and reflected the blue of its penetrating eyes. Conrad was not afraid, and the fear and pain within him just a short time ago vanished. He knelt beside him and looked into the wolf's eyes. In those ancient knowing eyes, he found courage and understanding.

Words came flowing from Conrad's mouth finding solace in the presence of Invictus.

Conrad had found peace, and the time with the wolf would be his redemption. And the night continued soft and inviting.

# Chapter 52

It was almost daybreak when Conrad found his way to Maureen's. There was no one at the front desk, but he called her and managed to say he was in trouble to please let him in. When she opened the door, she found him disheveled and exhausted but noted a quiet resolve. Harry was there to help her jockey him to the couch to lay down.

When he felt safe, he looked at his sister and confessed, he had so much to tell her. She hugged her brother tight and told him she loved him. She assured him they would talk later. He needed some rest.

"Get some sleep and I'll be here when you wake," she said.

Convinced he was secure with her, he fell quickly asleep. Maureen called the office and informed them she would be working from home, to take any messages and forward them to her. Maureen looked at her brother and then at Harry,

"It's starting, Harry. I can feel it. I haven't seen my brother like this in years. It's her hold over him. She has done it for years. When she married and was gone his career bloomed. He was not always like what he has become. Life was good when she was not around."

Anger was now infusing Maureen. She had seen the dark side of Nora more than once in her life. They were of the same blood and mother, but birth had separated the paths that each would take. Satan had taken Nora from them that minute after midnight. She no longer could be thought of as a blood sister. Maureen could feel the evil that emanated from Nora. There was disaster ahead and it was close.

She ran to her bedside to retrieve her bible. Harry looked on in complete confusion at her antics and angry demeanor. Hopelessly, she looked at Harry who was in quite the state,

"I know you don't understand all this, you're far too conventional. I love you for trying to understand, but to you, Nora is just a bad person up to no-good, but believe me, Harry, evil witches, demons, spells, and hexes are for real. I feel her, Harry, but I haven't been able to see what she will do."

Harry felt powerless. He tried to comfort her. "It's alright. It's alright, trying to soothe her agitation.

"No Harry, it's not alright. You do not know what she is capable of. Nora is not of this world, and I mean NOT OF THIS WORLD." She tried to emphasize this fact. "You do not want to experience her wrath."

Harry tried to take hold of what this woman he loved so deeply was saying. Maureen lovingly looked at Harry, trying so hard to make sense of things.

"Look, you go on to your office, I'll be here with him all day. I'll be OK, talk to Uncle John, update him on what has happened, and ask him to meet us here this evening." Maureen warned, "This dinner Friday to review his Will & Trust has triggered her. I'll see you later. Try not to worry."

Reluctantly, Harry went to the door, not wanting to leave her. It was only her insistence that found him at his office talking to Josh and Uncle John relaying the early morning circumstances. Speaking first to Josh, "Look, Josh, you got me into this, can you help me understand any of it. I know you told me you saw this thing that Maggie and you talked about at Garth and Zoe's house. I know the history of upstate New York, and all its headless horsemen and goblin rubbish, but I don't believe in such things. I believe in bad people doing bad things. Look, I checked out any vandalism or enemies that Zoe and Garth might have had. Frankly, I still find all that nonsense hard to believe."

Harry updated Josh about Conrad coming to Maureen's apartment, "When Maureen's brother showed up, she got all protective and started talking about things, not of this world."

"Harry, slow down," Josh said. "Before you go on rambling, let me call Zoe." Maybe it's time we had some reinforcements. I felt the same way you did before I talked to a priest. I'll call you back later. In the meantime, see if you can find anything else on our friend Johnny Polo."

Harry, unused to having things out of his control, put his hat in his hand for Josh's help, leaving it up to him. Now Johnny Polo, that was something he could sink his teeth into. He called Tiffany at his office and they both went to work on finding this charmer Polo.

About 4:00 p.m., Harry called to check on Maureen. He asked about Conrad. She sounded relieved. It was good to have her brother back in a way she had not seen him in a long time. Conrad had slept a good portion of the afternoon away. He had just started to stir about 10 minutes ago and she put on a pot of coffee for him.

Harry was glad to hear everything was quiet. He told her he had spoken to her Uncle John earlier, and let him know about Conrad. "Maureen, I don't want you to worry about anything tonight. I'll be there at about seven. There is somebody I want you to meet."

"Oh Harry, please Not tonight, I don't think that would be a very good idea."

Before her resistance became more vocal, He asked that she please trust him. Her mind was overwhelmed today. The last thing she needed was outside particulars interfering with the problems before her.

"Please trust me, Maureen," Harry beseeched. What could she say?"You take care of Conrad, and I'll see you at about seven."

It had been a busy day for many, and by seven that evening Joe greeted Harry and several others who appeared to be coming to Miss Maureen's for a "summit meeting"

Joe quickly buzzed Harry and the others up to the apartment, but not without a special treat from Harry, Rembrandt's signature dessert.

"See Joe it pays to know someone who owns a 4-star restaurant," remarked Harry.

Josh's investment in the fledgling restaurant had been rewarding.

When Maureen answered the door, she was lovingly greeted by her Uncle John, Harry, and Josh. Harry came bearing Rembrandt's finest culinary appetizers and specialties. He handed them to Maureen and took the initiative of introducing her to the one person she did not know, Father Michael Fitzhugh.

# Chapter 53

ather Mike immediately charmed his way into the hearts of Maureen and her brother. With his warm Irish brogue and disarming smile. He set them both at ease. While getting to know these two young people, he was not at all shy about requesting some of that "loovly" sherry that Josh kept talking about. Within 30 minutes Father Mike had them all entranced with his Irish stories. Maureen's apartment, which had been so beautifully appointed, but cold and lonely for so long, was filled with warmth and laughter. Even Max found the company of the old priest welcoming, as the dog lay comfortably at his feet. Most importantly, Harry saw the stress and high anxiety of Maureen completely banished from her face. How was it possible she could be more beautiful than when he first met this woman?

Harry never wanted to see such strain on her face again. He also saw another Conrad tonight. For this night, the swagger and disdain that only Harry knew, was absent. He saw the open and fresh face of a young man free of pretense and bluster. If nothing else the Father had given them relief for the night.

As Harry digested these thoughts, Father Mike picked up the Bible Maureen had set on the side table and looked directly at her.

"I understand you and your family are having difficulty dealing with a particular problem."

"I want you to know that I know these problems are real. You do not have to belong to a church or be of a certain faith to be targeted by such things. I have known of non-believers where such evil has visited."

Harry could have sworn Father Mike looked directly at him, and he realized, then, he had left his faith long ago.

"Now," he looked at John, Maureen, and Conrad, "we must get serious."

Father Mike dropped all pretense of the affable old Leprechaun of the old country. He was a huge man with broad shoulders, stood tall for a man of his age, and had a chest like a barrel. There was a strength and urgency in his voice.

"We fight. I want you to tell me everything you know about this THING. Father Mike placed his enormous hand, filled with warmth and love, on Conrad's shoulder.

"Now, my boy, you must tell me."

It was a cathartic gesture. Years of pain and fear spewed from Conrad's always silenced voice. His sister's transformations, threats, and spells. His self-loathing and confusion. His fear for his life, and family, and all of his puny resistance to stop her. He spoke of the wolf last night, and its ability to give him courage. He rose, went to his uncle, and hugged him.

"Uncle John, she wants you dead." Conrad broke down in his uncle's arms. John hugged the boy close and reassured him of his love. Growing hate for Nora fueled his desire to destroy the evil within her. He turned to the priest for guidance.

Harry was happy Josh had convinced him to meet with him. Maureen stood by experiencing the pain and loss Nora had visited on this family. If she had gone away and stayed away, she thought, they all might not be living this nightmare.

Finally, she said, "I don't possess the powers Nora has, but I do know something terrible is about to happen. She can't hide from me. I feel what and when she feels and the evil is growing. You must stay away from her Uncle John."

For the first time, Maureen did not have to face this alone. She looked at Harry, John, and Father Fitzhugh, and tranquility and strength flowed through her.

Father Mike took her by the hand and sat down, "Come now, we must speak of certain things. There is much to be done to draw her out. Plans must be made." Father Mike, Conrad, Maureen, and John sat together, and a conspiracy began.

Josh excused himself, and Harry saw him to the door. Maggie would be waiting for him. He had been through a similar story before.

# Chapter 54

An unlikely alliance between believer and non-believer was forged that night. Harry delivered Father Mike to the rectory well after midnight. Harry was not a spiritual man, but he was a good man. He found himself oddly in sync with this priest. There was a realness about him. His reluctance to accept such things as true love, God, and the devil were being tested. Hard-nosed Harry and the wall around him was beginning to crumble. He called Maureen to say he had safely delivered the Father and that he loved her. Without hesitation, she softly echoed his sentiment and thanked him and Josh for bringing Father Fitzhugh to them.

Conrad and Uncle John were staying another night. Conrad was already asleep on the couch and Uncle John was in the guest room. They all felt it best that he did not spend the night at home. They all needed a good night's sleep.

Tomorrow, things will be set in motion.

# Chapter 55

Uncle John left Maureen's apartment early that morning to go home. Conrad was still sleeping calmly and they both agreed to let him sleep. Maureen had slept soundly and was finishing her second cup of coffee when Harry called. He did not sleep well and hoped this lunatic merry-go-round would come to an end today.

Harry had arranged to pick up Father Mike about noon. By that time John should have talked to Nora to inform him of his plans, and Conrad and Maureen should be there shortly after. If they were to draw this thing out, it would be today and all would present a united front.

John knew he was the lynchpin and bait. His announcement of Maureen heading the company and subsequent executor of his will and trust triggered her murderous intent.

Nora however, this morning, had no intention of unmasking her ulterior motives. She greeted her uncle sweetly this morning, offering up her kindest attendance.

"Would you like some more coffee Uncle John? There is also some fresh banana bread in the kitchen. I bought it early this morning from the village. I know it's your favorite."

John was agreeable this morning, but all business. He declined her offer and invited her into his study, something he had not done in quite some time. She sat obediently in the chair in front of the desk awaiting his next words.

"Nora, I'm thinking of taking an extended vacation. As you know, it has not been the same without your Aunt Diane here. You know how you felt after your parents." She bowed her head shamelessly in mock regret.

"I have talked to Maureen, and she has agreed to take a leave of absence from her employ. They assure her, her position will be waiting for her. I want to be fair to both of you, but she has far more business experience than you."

"But Uncle John." She leaned forward in a soft contrite voice, thinking she had successfully held the demon at bay, unaware that John experienced every hidden dagger of malfeasance she issued.

"I was so hoping my small involvement in the company this summer would prove my commitment to you and the family business. I know I could be an asset to you. Perhaps we could make some temporary changes until I've proven myself. I'm sure Maureen does not want to leave her job. She loves it. And I'm completely committed to Bradford Air." Nora could only hope this masquerade would buy her time in getting the business properly signed over temporarily to avoid probate and litigation. John did not answer her; he simply rose and went to the doors leading to his wife's greenhouse.

He turned to her and replied, completely off-topic, how his wife loved this greenhouse.

She had lost him, the old fool was meandering. Any manipulation was futile now, lost in his confounded memories of his simpering Diane.

John opened the doors and stepped out into the moist cocoon of his beloved wife's greenhouse. As Nora rose to follow him, Conrad and Maureen appeared at the study door. She brought Max along just to visit Uncle John. He had enjoyed the dog's company so much last night. Max was way ahead of any greeting. He bounded through the French doors to catch up with John, leaving the three siblings to themselves. There was scarcely an exchange between them before Nora's eyes locked eyes with a defiant Conrad. Seeing him with Maureen, she understood the implications. He had made his choice, and his allegiance to her had the impact of Thor's hammer. A silent roar welled within her. All pretense was abandoned. She alone would dismiss the petty defiance of the humans.

Nora's anger unleashed all the dark powers within her, arousing them to visit torment and destruction on those who defied her. Her disintegrating human form growing in strength and power exploded through the greenhouse doors dwarfing the figure of John Bradford and the dog.

John stood his ground, mesmerized but defiant. The towering, bloating body of flesh, taking its time in its alteration. It saw Conrad and Maureen looking on and shrieked its displeasure. No longer a vestige of human form visible, the shrieking mass of demon extended formless, threatening arms of hellfire toward John. The stench as it grew closer sickened both man and dog. Conrad and Maureen advanced, shielding John, unwilling to fall back. With heavenly resolve, a thunderous noise, far greater than the demon, shook the foundation of the greenhouse.

The horror unfolding ushered in the arrival of the old priest with his bible and cross in hand caught up in a whirlwind of God's wrath and fury, shouting incantations at the hellion's onslaught. Harry looked on in disbelief and amazement at the priest when the appearance of Invictus, the large grey wolf, lunged forward in defiance of the advancing evil. The animal's head was bowed low with bristling hackles of steel, emitting a deep and primeval growl. The guttural warning shook Harry to his very core.

The sky grew dark, and Invictus moved forward, daring the mass to proceed. His fangs glistened as he advanced with a fierceness in his eyes that momentarily hindered its progress. The demon grew in strength and power, the wolf howled to the heavens, and the heavens responded. Father Mike stood tall with the bible held high, his powerful voice invoking all that was sacred and banishing all forces of evil. The heavens cried, and the sky grew black as the greenhouse trembled as the wolf gave warning, and all man and animal retreated to safety. Rolling thunder echoed, and the lightning danced in a fractured seizure of a macabre terpsichore. Mid-morning had fallen into complete darkness and as if on cue, in perfect timing. A single bolt of God's fury lit up the sky destroying the evil beneath the glass dome.  The giant glass enclosure erupted in millions of glass shards plummeting to the earth in tinkling musical destruction.

All became silent.

# Chapter 56

The vibrancy of the morning returned. The sun burned warm and inviting, bidding the birds return to song, and the stunned participants in this unearthly play slowly returned to normalcy, forever changed from the experience. The group stood wordless for the moment, and a disquieted Harry, legs trembling, found a rock wall to sit down and recoup. Maureen quickly followed. Father Mike, Conrad, and Uncle John stayed clustered, watching as the wolf encircled the smoldering mass that once had been in human guise moments ago. Max watched quietly as his ancient kinsman surveyed the area.

Content that for the moment, all evil and darkness had been removed from this site, Invictus turned his attention to the humans before him. It was then that Harry found himself face to face with the animal. A momentary fear froze Harry to the rock wall, but immediately dissipated when he looked into the animal's eyes. A kinship was born. He touched the great silver head and the introduction was complete. That day, it was guaranteed that Harry Quinn's life would never be the same.

Moments passed and then a silent goodbye passed between man and beast. Invictus then turned to the old priest and the others, and in silent acknowledgment, indicated his job was complete. He turned, focusing his attention elsewhere. The distant hillside beckoned him with the soft sounds of windchimes carried on gentle breezes. The old warrior wolf was being summoned. As a sign of respect, Max escorted his revered ancestor to the hillside, and they all watched as he disappeared beyond their sight.

The day was magic.

# Chapter 57

A slack-jawed Harry finally arose from his sitting position. Maureen beside him seemed to help him up.

"What just happened here?" he asked no one in particular. "Where the hell is Captain Hook and Tinkerbell? Because I sure as hell know I'm in Never-never-land."

Father Mike chuckled. As did Uncle John and Conrad, as all had encountered the pleasure of the wolf's company before. Harry had heard about it but really didn't believe it. Not really. He still wasn't sure.

Father Mike simply looked at Harry and said, There are some things in life we just do not question, my boy. The leprechaun had returned. The priest from the land of the little people had just given sage advice.

There was no way Harry could explain what just happened. He looked at Maureen, who had been strangely quiet through this unfolding drama. When the realization of what just happened hit her, it brought tears of happiness. She threw her arms around Harry and squeezed him tight.

"Do you know what this means? No more nightmares, no more living in fear. No more, she thought for a minute, Evil. No more sister. The enormity of what she just said took hold. "Freedom."

She and Conrad were free. She looked at her brother and then her uncle. It was good to see them together, in a way she hadn't seen them in a long time. She reached out to Father Mike and shook his hand, thanking him for all he had done. Maureen had shouldered this secret burden alone for many years. She again turned her attention to Uncle John and Conrad, together, looking as if they had never been closer.

The dark side of what had been living in their midst had been exposed. John was unaware of such evil and Conrad was a prisoner of it. The shocked fivesome seemed to regroup and assess the damage. John thought of his beloved wife Diane, and how much she loved her greenhouse, how she had died tending it. The evil that took his Diane ironically ended here by divine intervention.

"Nothing that can't be replaced," he said. We'll build it bigger and better. Diane would like that. Now let's all go back to the house and have a wee bit of my special reserve. What do you say, Father?"

"Don't mind if I do John, it's been a very trying day."

"Oh, and Maureen, I want my dog back. That means you'll be moving back here. Got any problems with that?"

"Not at all Uncle John, Not at all."

"Come on Max, let's go inside."

Maureen turned and found Harry had broken from the group inspecting the debris left behind.

"What are you doing?"

"Oh nothing, just looking,"

"Looking for what?

Harry looked at her and couldn't believe he was going to say what he was going to say.

"TheWolf" heaved and rolled his eyes. The wolf said, I mean, communicated to me to check the remains. Maureen looked at him and giggled.

"You mean the wolf talked to you?"

"Noooo... forget it, let's go in. Just then the green stones flashed fire. Harry reached down carefully avoiding the residue of tiny glass shards to retrieve an intricately carved emerald bracelet from the collection of Satan's Fire.

Harry Quinn had become a believer in fairy tales, elves....

and a Divine Power.

# Epilogue

Johnny Polo was under no delusions. He was on the run. It had been a hell of a ride since snatching the jewels, but the stolen gems were far too hot and valuable to be forgotten. His contacts were small-time fences, and he did not know what the islands had to offer.

Partying and casual alliances had to stop. Johnny had been lucky so far, but soon every insurance sleuth, cop, and street snitch would know about Satan's Fire. Worse yet, Johnny Polo had no idea Harry Quinn was not far behind.